THIS IGLOO BOOK BELONGS TO:

MATLEYMEVE

igloobooks

Published in 2015
by Igloo Books Ltd
Cottage Farm
Sywell
NN6 0BJ
www.igloobooks.com

SHE001 0715
2 4 6 8 10 9 7 5 3 1
ISBN: 978-1-78440-981-4

Printed and manufactured in China

My Ultimate DreamWorks Treasury

CONTENTS

SHREK

MADAGASCAR

MONSTERS VS ALIENS

KUNG FU PANDA

THE CROODS

PENGUINS

HOME

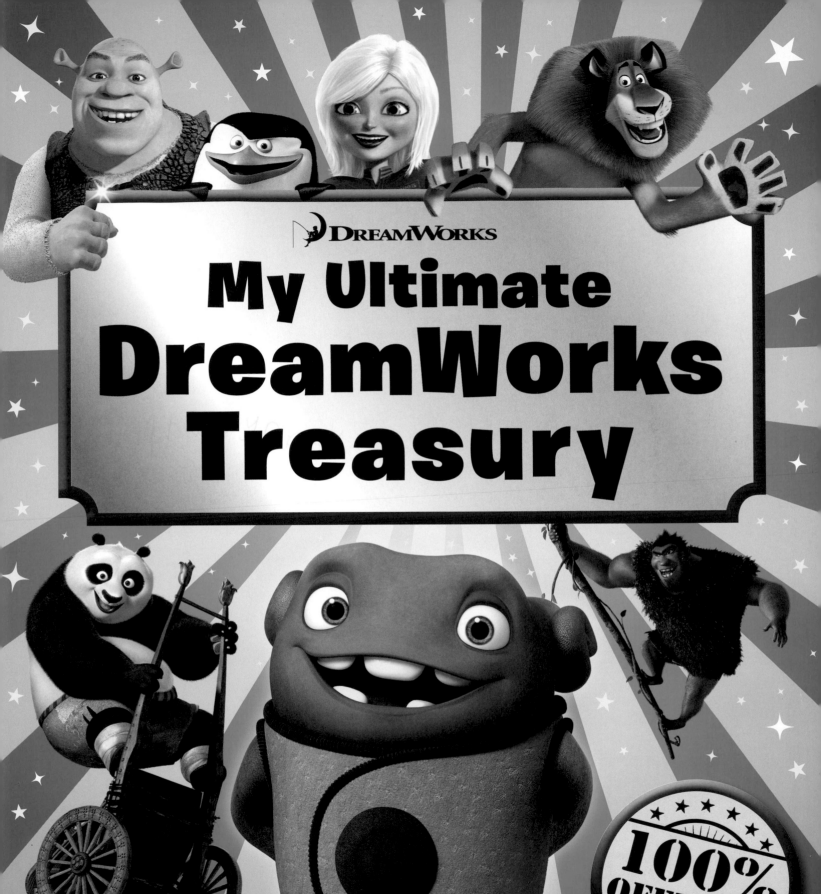

DreamWorks

My Ultimate DreamWorks Treasury

100% OFFICIAL

igloobooks

SHREK

In a land far, far away lived an ogre called Shrek. He loved being big, smelly and, most importantly, alone. However, all that changed when he bumped into a chatty donkey in the woods.

"I think you and I are going to be great friends," Donkey said, grinning.

When Shrek arrived home, followed by the annoyingly talkative Donkey, he found his swamp was overrun with lots of fairy-tale folk.

"Why are you all here?" cried Shrek, angrily.

"It's Lord Farquaad!" squealed a little pig. "He forced us to leave DuLoc."

Shrek was furious! He decided to have a loud word with Lord Farquaad.

Meanwhile in DuLoc, Lord Farquaad was talking to his Magic Mirror. "Mirror, mirror, on the wall, is this not the most perfect kingdom of them all?" The Magic Mirror reflected. "It cannot truly be a kingdom for it has no king," it said. Then, the Mirror showed Farquaad three princesses and explained that, by marrying one, he would become the King of DuLoc.

Farquaad chose a beautiful princess named Fiona, but there was a dragon guarding her. "Hmm," schemed the cowardly Lord Farquaad. "I'll hold a tournament and the champion will win the 'honour' of rescuing her for me!"

Shrek and Donkey arrived in DuLoc just as the tournament was beginning in the stadium.

As Shrek walked in, Farquaad thought up a new plan. "He who kills the ogre will be named champion," he announced.

Knights charged Shrek. His only choice was to fight. The crowd gasped as he knocked down every knight, one after the other.

"Congratulations, Ogre," said Farquaad. "You've won the honour of embarking on a great quest." Shrek just wanted his swamp back. "I'll make you a deal," said Farquaad. "Rescue Princess Fiona and I'll return your swamp." Shrek agreed.

Shrek grabbed a suit of armour and the two friends left DuLoc.
"I don't get it, Shrek," said Donkey. "Why didn't you pull some of that
ogre stuff? You know, grind Farquaad's bones to make your bread."
"There's a lot more to ogres than people think," answered Shrek. "Ogres are
like onions. They both have layers."

Before long, the flowery fields of DuLoc gave way to a barren wasteland
of dark jagged rocks and a pungent odour filled the air.
"It's brimstone," said Shrek. "We must be getting close to the dragon."

Up ahead stood a blackened castle perched over a molten lava lake. "I'll handle the dragon, you go find some stairs. The princess will be in the tallest tower," said Shrek. Donkey was glad he didn't have to look for the dragon, the stairs were scary enough for him.

As Donkey crept down the dark hallway, he rounded a corner and found himself facing the massive red dragon! He fled, as the dragon blew out a fireball. Shrek arrived just in time and shoved Donkey out of the fireball's blazing path.

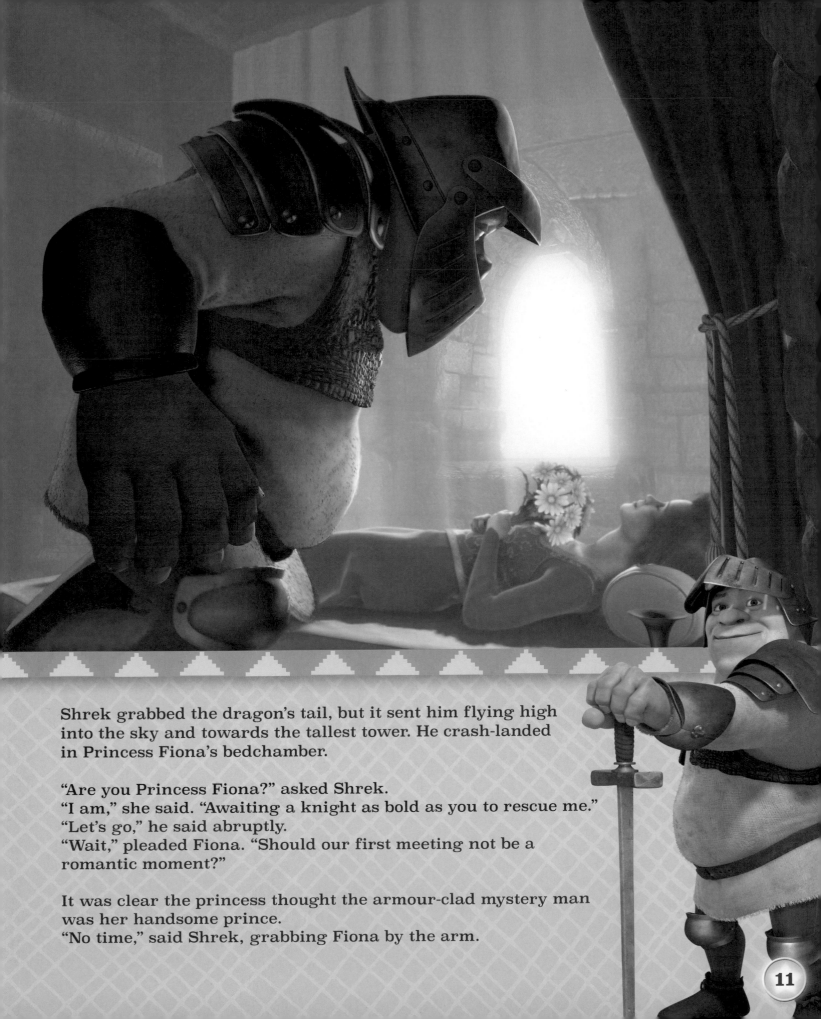

Shrek grabbed the dragon's tail, but it sent him flying high into the sky and towards the tallest tower. He crash-landed in Princess Fiona's bedchamber.

"Are you Princess Fiona?" asked Shrek.
"I am," she said. "Awaiting a knight as bold as you to rescue me."
"Let's go," he said abruptly.
"Wait," pleaded Fiona. "Should our first meeting not be a romantic moment?"

It was clear the princess thought the armour-clad mystery man was her handsome prince.
"No time," said Shrek, grabbing Fiona by the arm.

11

Meanwhile, Donkey decided to do what he did best - talk.
"What large white teeth you have," he chattered. The dragon batted its eyelashes and Donkey realised it was a girl dragon. He'd flirt his way out of danger!

Just as the dragon pursed her lips for a kiss, Shrek swung on a nearby chain and tried to grab Donkey. THWUMP! Shrek missed. He let go of the chain and the end of it came crashing down, landing like a collar around the dragon's huge neck. Shrek, Donkey and Fiona ran.

Safely away from danger, Fiona turned to Shrek.
"You rescued me!" she cried. Her fairy-tale was finally coming true.

Now it was time for the kiss she'd been waiting for. Fiona demanded
that Shrek remove his helmet. As he did, she just stared.
"You're... an ogre?" she asked.
"I was sent to rescue you by Lord Farquaad. He wants to marry you,"
explained Shrek.
"Well, then tell him to rescue me!" she snapped.
"I'm a delivery boy, not a messenger boy,"
said Shrek, as he flung Fiona over his shoulder.

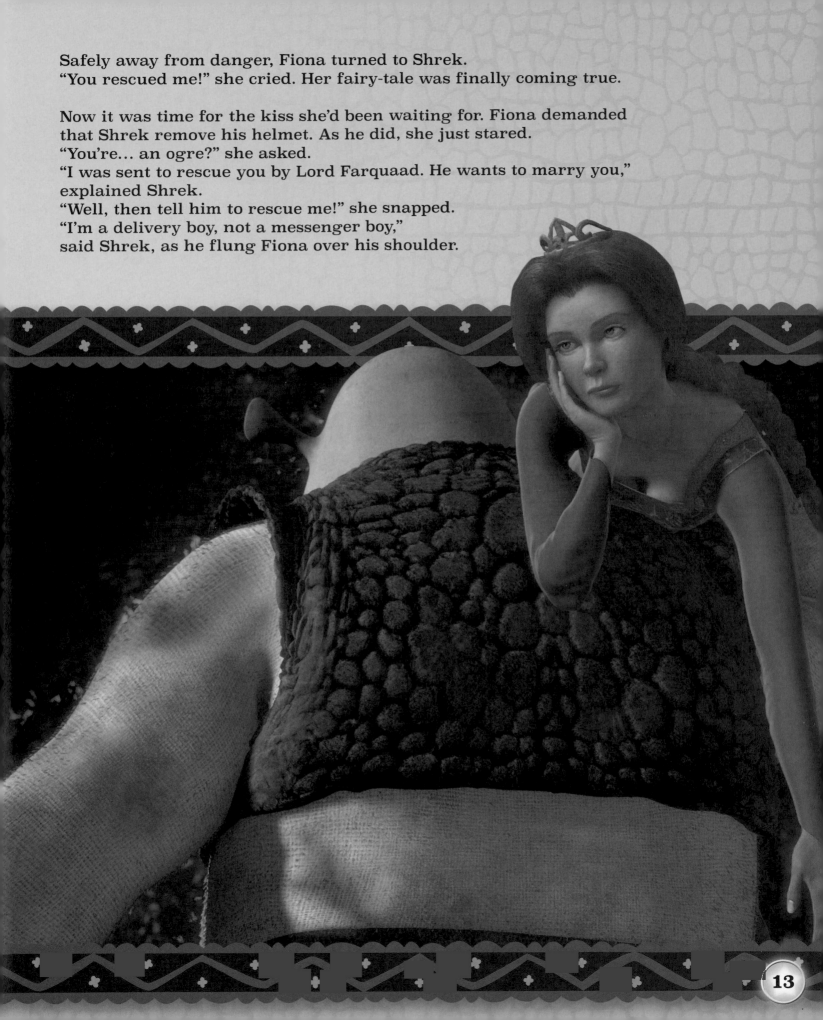

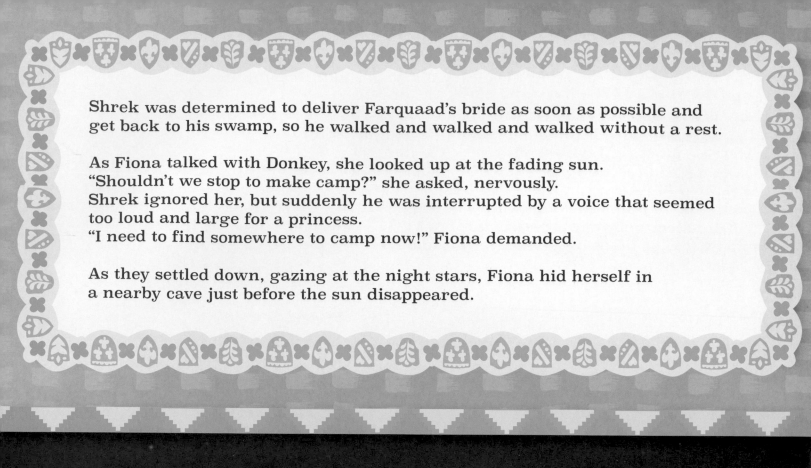

Shrek was determined to deliver Farquaad's bride as soon as possible and get back to his swamp, so he walked and walked and walked without a rest.

As Fiona talked with Donkey, she looked up at the fading sun.
"Shouldn't we stop to make camp?" she asked, nervously.
Shrek ignored her, but suddenly he was interrupted by a voice that seemed too loud and large for a princess.
"I need to find somewhere to camp now!" Fiona demanded.

As they settled down, gazing at the night stars, Fiona hid herself in a nearby cave just before the sun disappeared.

In the morning the trio set off again. They hadn't been walking long when a man in green leaped from a branch and swept Fiona into a tree. "I'm Robin Hood and I'm rescuing you from this green beast," he declared. He jumped to the ground and called his Merry Men. Shrek was outnumbered.

"Hiyaaaah!" Fiona leaped into action. Within minutes, she had knocked out Robin and all of his men. Shrek and Donkey looked on, stunned and amazed at the princess' outburst.

As they continued on their journey, Donkey noticed that Shrek had been shot with one of Robin Hood's arrows. "Shrek's hurt!" panicked Donkey. "He's going to die."

Fiona remained calm and removed the arrow carefully. After that, Fiona and Shrek spent the rest of the day doing nice things for each other. Fiona whipped up a cotton-candy-like treat made of cobwebs and bugs for Shrek and he returned her gift with one of his own, a frog he inflated into a balloon. They were having so much fun together that they were no longer in a hurry to see Lord Farquaad.

That afternoon, they made camp by an old mill and Shrek cooked up his speciality, weedrat.

"Ummm, delicious," said Fiona, wolfing it down.

The princess and ogre gazed at each other.

"Isn't this romantic?" Donkey interrupted. "Just look at that sunset."

Fiona looked up, said a quick goodnight and raced into the mill.

"I know you two were digging each other," said Donkey to Shrek.

"Just go tell her how you feel."

"There's nothing to tell," said Shrek. "She's a princess and I'm an ogre."

Donkey crept into the mill to talk to Fiona, but was surprised to see an ogress!
"It's me!" hushed Fiona. "A witch cast a spell on me. Every night I become this
horrible beast. That's why I have to marry Farquaad. Only true love's first
kiss can break the spell."
"What if you married Shrek, instead?" suggested Donkey.
"Look at me, Donkey," she said.

At that moment, Shrek approached the mill door.
"Who could ever love a beast so hideous and ugly?"
Shrek thought she was talking about him and walked away, sadly.

The next morning, Shrek stomped up to Princess Fiona.
"I've brought you a little something," he sneered. It was Lord Farquaad and his army! Shrek snatched the deed to his swamp and stormed off. "Princess," said Farquaad. "Will you be the perfect bride for the perfect groom?"

Fiona shot an angry glance at Shrek. "Let's get married today, Farquaad," she said, faking a smile. Farquaad agreed.

He and Fiona rode off together and Donkey, with an anxious last look at Fiona, hurried after Shrek.

Back home at the swamp, Donkey was talking to Shrek.
"You're afraid of your own feelings, onion boy," said Donkey. "All Fiona ever
did was like you. Maybe even love you."
"She said I was ugly!" replied Shrek.
"What? When? In the mill? She wasn't talking about you!" cried Donkey.

Shrek realised he had made a mistake. "I have to stop the wedding, Donkey!"
he cried.

Donkey whistled and Dragon swooped in.
"We've er… stayed in touch," said Donkey, smiling.
"I guess it's just my animal magnetism."

As the dragon soared over DuLoc, the wedding ceremony had started. Fiona glanced at the setting sun. "Could we just skip ahead to the end?" she asked. Farquaad stepped toward Fiona to kiss her.

Just then, Shrek burst in.
"I object!" he roared. "He's just marrying you to be king, Fiona." He charged towards the altar. "He's not your true love," said Shrek, looking deeply into Fiona's eyes. Lord Farquaad laughed.
"The ogre has fallen in love with the princess."
"Is this true?" Fiona asked, stepping forward.

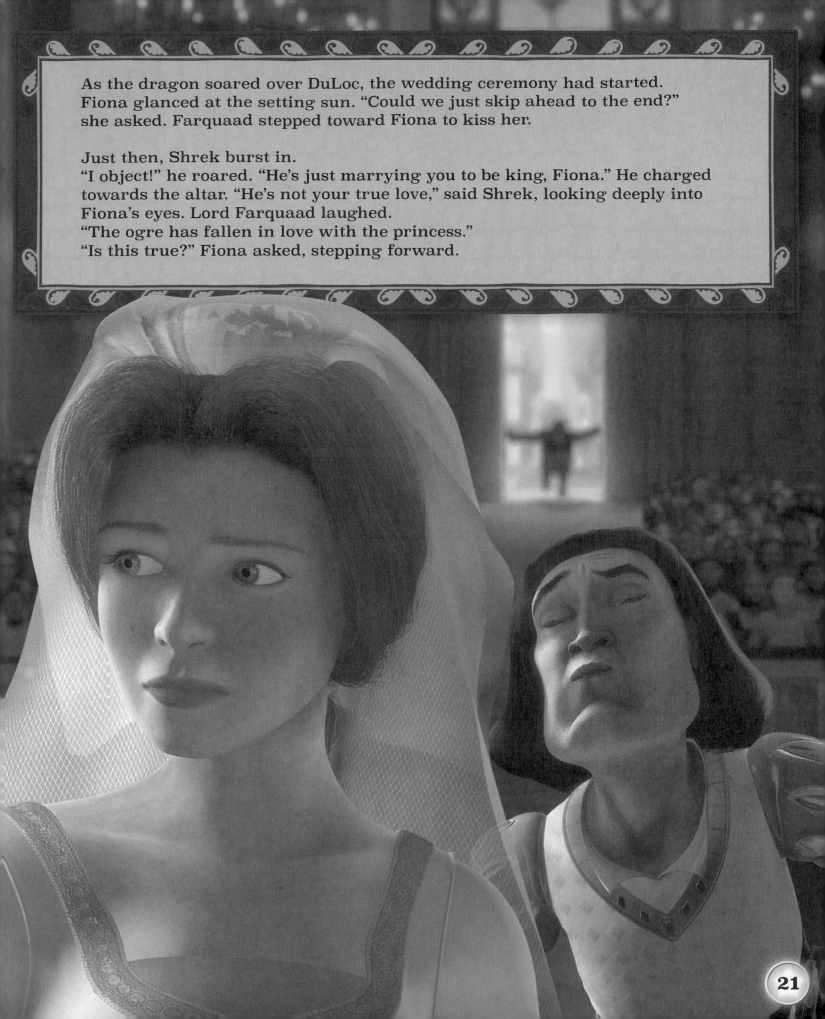

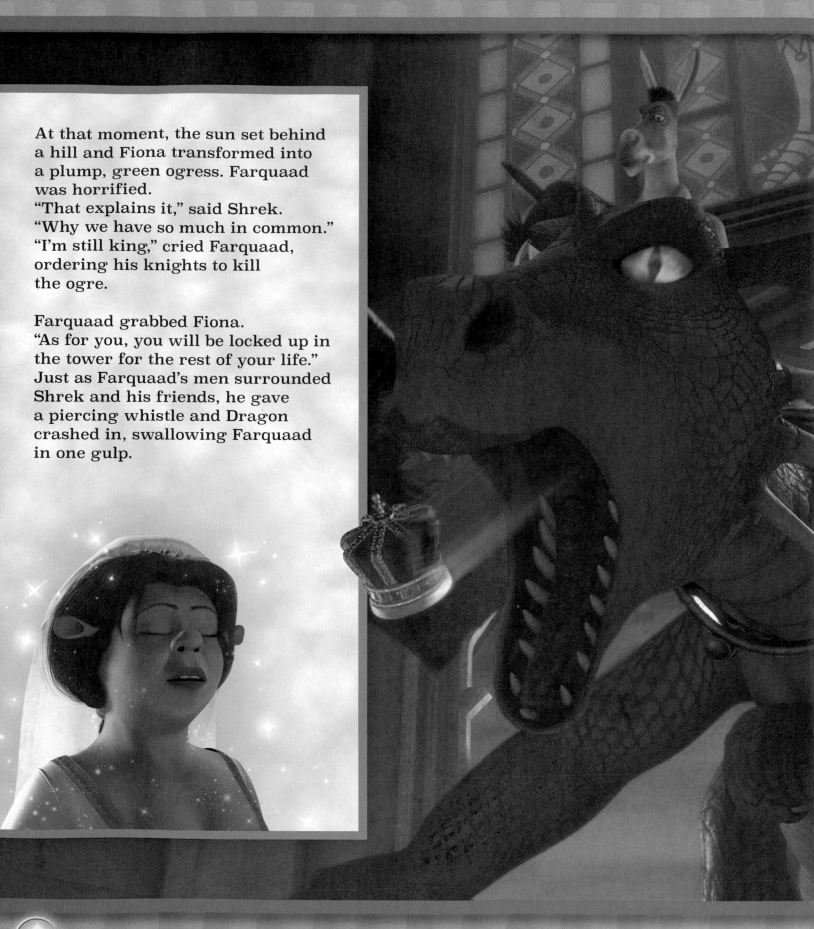

At that moment, the sun set behind
a hill and Fiona transformed into
a plump, green ogress. Farquaad
was horrified.
"That explains it," said Shrek.
"Why we have so much in common."
"I'm still king," cried Farquaad,
ordering his knights to kill
the ogre.

Farquaad grabbed Fiona.
"As for you, you will be locked up in
the tower for the rest of your life."
Just as Farquaad's men surrounded
Shrek and his friends, he gave
a piercing whistle and Dragon
crashed in, swallowing Farquaad
in one gulp.

Shrek turned to the princess.

"Fiona," he said. "I love you."

"I love you, too," Fiona replied. They kissed and the ogress floated into the air and was shrouded in flashing light.

Finally, Fiona fell to the floor. The crowd waited in suspense to discover what love's true form would be. When Fiona rose again, she was still an ogress.

"I don't understand. I'm supposed to be beautiful."

"You look beautiful to me," said Shrek. "Marry me?"

"Yes!" cried Fiona.

And they lived together, happily ever after.

MADAGASCAR

DREAM**W**ORKS

At the New York Zoo, Marty the zebra was bored. As he sat and wondered if anything exciting was ever going to happen, a penguin popped up through the ground in his pen. Marty watched, puzzled, as three more penguins suddenly appeared.

"Hey, stripy. Is this the wild?" said Skipper, the penguins' leader. Marty shook his head. "Kowalski, plot a new course," ordered Skipper. "To the train station! The wild here we come." "You can go there?" asked Marty. "It really exists?" Before he got an answer, the penguins were gone.

That night, Alex the lion, Gloria the hippo and
Melman the giraffe had a birthday party for Marty.
"Make a wish," said Gloria, handing Marty a cake.
He thought for a moment and then blew out the candles.

"What did you wish for?" asked Alex.
"To go to the wild!" announced Marty.
"Listen," said Alex. "Everyone has days when they
think the grass might be greener somewhere else."
"I just feel there's more to being a zebra than this,"
sighed Marty.

Later that night, Melman looked into Marty's pen.
He was gone!
"Alex! Wake up. Marty isn't here!" he cried.
"Where would he go?" asked Gloria.
"He was talking about the wild last night, but he
wouldn't have. He couldn't have. Could he?" replied Alex.
"We've got to find him."

The three friends busted out of the zoo and raced to the
train station. Even the penguins were there, excited to
go to the wild.

At the station, people were running and screaming at
the top of their voices everywhere.
"It's an animal attack!" they cried. "Run for your lives!"
Alex searched the busy station and soon saw Marty.
"Do you realise what you put us through?" asked Alex,
shaking Marty. "Don't you ever do this again!"

Suddenly, masses of policemen in riot gear swarmed the hall. Alex tried to explain, but it was too late. A tranquilizer dart hit him on the leg and before he could do anything he fell asleep.

Some time later, the four friends and the penguins woke up in wooden crates.
"Oh, no! It's a zoo transfer," groaned Alex.
"Calm down," cried Marty from another crate.
"We are going to be o-kizzay."
"Don't tell me to calm down," roared Alex.
"This is all your fault!"

THE WILD

Alex and Marty started shoving the walls of their crates, trying to push each other's over. As they banged around, all of the other crates began to rock. Suddenly... SPLASH! The crates toppled overboard into the sea. The penguins, who were also on the ship, seized their opportunity, picked the lock on their crate and were soon in control of the ship.

Meanwhile, the crates with Alex and his friends bobbed on the waves until finally, they washed up on the shore of an island. Marty burst out of his crate. He liked what he saw.
"This place is crack-a-lackin', you guys!" he cried.

Alex looked around. Suddenly, just beyond the trees at the edge of the beach, music started to play. The four friends followed the sound into the jungle. As they entered a clearing, they saw animals everywhere.
"What kind of zoo is this?" asked Gloria.
A lemur named Maurice emerged from the jungle.
"Presenting your Royal Highness, King Julien the thirteenth!" he cheered.

Julien marched out of the bushes.
"He's got style," whispered Marty.
"Welcome… to the wild!" said Julien.
"The wild?" cried Alex in disbelief.

Marty's birthday wish had come true.
"We're in the wild! We're in the wild!" he yelled. "This could be the best thing that's ever happened to us."

Alex didn't think so. In fact, he was sure that it was the worst thing that had ever happened to him. All he could do was hope for a rescue boat.

Back on the ship, the penguins celebrated as they headed toward Antarctica.
"It's going to be ice-cold sushi for breakfast, boys!" cried Skipper.

As the sun set on the island, Alex and Marty were arguing.
Alex drew a line in the sand.
"This is your side of the island and this is our side, for those who love New York and care about going home."
"Fine," said Marty. "You have your side and I have mine. If you need me, I'll be over here, on the fun side."

Melman rolled his eyes and rubbed two sticks together.
Seconds later, sparks began to fly and the sticks caught fire, making him jump!
"Can we go to the fun side now?" he asked.

Eventually, after Alex had watched Marty
enjoying life on the fun side, he gave in and
joined him. Gloria and Melman were already
there with Marty in his cosy hut.

"I've been a jerk," said Alex to Marty. "If this
is what you want, then I'll give it a shot."
"Welcome to Casa del Wild," smiled Marty.

The four friends spent the rest of the evening
eating seaweed kebabs. The only thing that
was missing was Alex's favourite food, steak.
He couldn't think about anything else.

Elsewhere on the island, King Julien and the lemurs were having a meeting.
"We should make the large animals from New York our friends," said one lemur.
"For as long as we can remember, we've been attacked and eaten by the fossa,"
said Julien. "With Alex protecting us, we'll be safe and never have to worry again!"
"Yay!" the lemurs shouted.
"The New York giants will wake up in paradise tomorrow!" yelled Julien.
"They will never want to leave!"

Meanwhile, the penguins had finally reached Antarctica, but it was too cold!
They set sail again for somewhere warm.

The next morning, King Julien was making sure that the four friends felt truly welcomed. He had prepared a delicious breakfast of fruits and vegetables for them.

After breakfast, Marty decided to go for a run. "Who's with me?" he asked.

Alex started running, with Marty in hot pursuit. The pair dashed through the wild, tackling each other and having fun.

By the time they returned to the waterhole, Alex was feeling better and wilder than he'd ever felt before.

Later that day, Marty and Alex put on a show unlike any that they had ever done before.
"Ladies and gentlemen, the wild proudly presents the king: Alex the lion!"

Alex leaped onto a rock and, for the first time in his life, really ROARED.
"Whoa," said Gloria. "I never heard that sound from him before."
The locals began cheering.

Alex's act was brilliant, but he couldn't stop smelling steak and it was making him really hungry. He opened his mouth to let out another roar, but tried to bite Marty instead!

The crowd gasped and Marty jumped back. There was only one thing to do.
"Your friend is what you'd call a deluxe hunting-and-eating machine," King Julien
explained. "Mr Alex belongs with his own kind, on the other side of the island."

Everyone stared at Alex, who began to back away into the jungle, until he
disappeared. Marty was confused.
"This isn't how the wild is supposed to be," he said, as he stared after his friend.

Marty was sad.

"Don't worry, we'll figure this out," said Gloria. BRAAAAP!

"Gloria!" said Melman, embarrassed.

"That wasn't me, okay. That was the boat. The boat!"

"Flag it down!" shouted Marty.

They ran down to the beach, waving and calling. The boat began to turn towards them.

"It's coming back! It's coming back!" screamed Gloria.

"You guys hold the boat. I'll go get Alex," said Marty, running back into the jungle.

As an anchor thudded into the sand, the penguins slid down the chain and landed next to Gloria and Melman.

Across the island, deep in the jungle, Marty found Alex.
"Alex! The boat is here! We can go home!"
"Stay away!" said Alex. "I'm a monster."
"No," replied Marty. "You're the best friend a guy could have and I'm not leaving without you." Alex looked at Marty, turned and walked away.

As Marty reluctantly made his way back to the boat, he was surrounded by a fierce pack of fossa. Marty took one look at the hungry pack and ran, but there were too many of them and soon he was trapped.

Suddenly, a yell rang through the trees. Melman flew through the air, swinging on a vine like Tarzan. He grabbed Marty and carried him safely out of reach. Gloria was waiting for them and the three friends ran away as fast as they could.

The animal pack raced after them, but just as they were getting closer, Skipper and his troops appeared. A fierce battle erupted with the penguins, the lemurs and the three friends fighting side by side, but they were heavily outnumbered by the fossa.

Just when it looked like the fierce pack would win, an almighty roar brought the fight to a sudden stop.

Alex leaped into the middle of the brawl and showed off his incredibly sharp claws. Marty, Melman, Gloria and the penguins looked on, amazed.
"It's show time," he said, winking at his friends. Then, he turned to face the pack.

"I never, ever want to see you on my turf again!" he roared at the terrified creatures, who didn't wait any longer. They turned and ran away into the jungle.

That afternoon, there was a huge party to celebrate. Music played and the penguins made sushi... which Alex even tried! It wasn't steak, but he liked it a lot.

As the four friends looked around at the locals and the penguins, they realised that it didn't matter where they were, as long as they were together. Marty's dream of living in the wild had come true, but best of all he and Alex were friends again.

With that they all raised their coconut cups and toasted.
"Here's to a new life... here in the wild!"

An alien craft has landed in the middle of the US desert.
"No one knows what it is, or where it came from," states a news reporter.

The reporter continues...

"I have just received word that the President of the United States has arrived and will attempt to make first contact."

As news of the new visitor was breaking across the world, a fleet of helicopters filled up the sky.

President Hathaway, flanked by a team of aides in dark suits, emerged from the helicopters ready to come face-to-face with the huge foreigner who had landed from outer space.

The president gulped and slowly made his way towards the alien ship. He had no idea what to expect from the alien. The president approached a keyboard, which had been set up for him and began to play a popular and welcoming melody in a bid to show the alien he meant peace.

Through an opening door on the alien ship, a large robotic hand emerges as if to shake the president's hand – then BAM! – it smashed the instrument.

The president quickly drew back and an army commander, who had been watching the exchange, immediately ordered his soldiers to take action.

"Light 'em up," he barked to his army.

A tidal wave of bullets, rockets and missiles aimed at the robot soared through the sky, but the ammunition simply bounced off the robot's force field.

Barely containing the panic in his voice, the army commander ordered his troops to immediately retreat. It had very quickly become apparent that the military wouldn't be able to take down this alien invader. It was time to call upon the government's special secret weapons...

... MONSTERS! General Monger knew Earth's only chance of survival was the motley crew of mutants he kept locked up in a top secret prison. He promised the monsters their freedom if they helped defeat the evil robot who was causing destruction everywhere.

One of the monsters, Ginormica, a woman who transformed into a giant on her wedding day when she was hit by a meteorite, carefully considered General Monger's proposal.

Susan – otherwise known as Ginormica, wanted her old, normal size back. So, she set about hatching a plan with the other monsters, B.O.B. an indestructible blob, the mad scientist Dr Cockroach, The Missing Link who was an ancient fish-man and Insectosaurus, a huge grub.

The group arrived in San Francisco ready to face the alien robot, but he spotted them first and charged at Ginormica, chasing her towards the centre of the city.

B.O.B decided to take action and stuck himself to the robot's foot in a bid to slow him down. However, the robot simply carried on with his rampage through the city.

Next, it was up to Dr Cockroach to try and defeat the mighty robot.

"I have a plan," he cried, having spotted a nearby tram. "To the untrained eye, a tram is just a tram, but to a genius, it's a foundation for a turbo-powered vehicle."

He quickly got to work creating the powerful machine.

Dr Cockroach and The Missing Link chased after the robot. Dr Cockroach ordered The Missing Link to try to access the robot's central processing unit.

However, B.O.B accidentally got in the way and ended up splatting across the entire windscreen of the tram, causing it to crash into the water.

Meanwhile, the interstellar invader was still on Ginormica's trail. He crashed through buildings and trampled down trees in his bid to catch her.

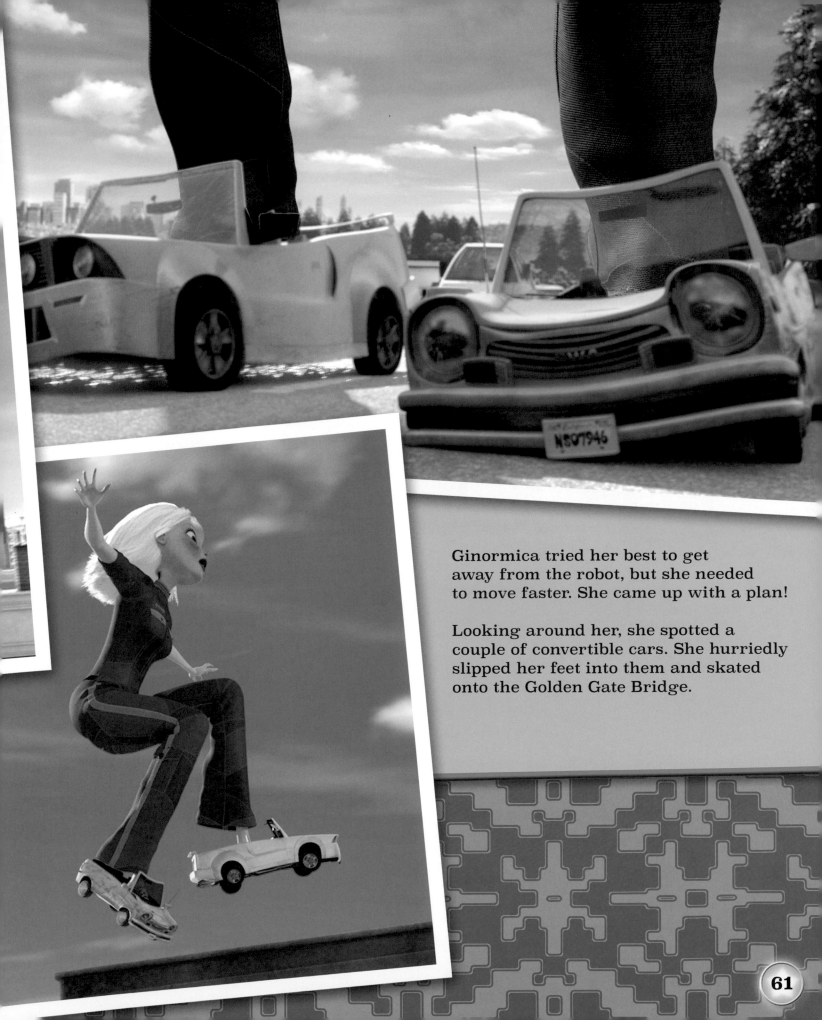

Ginormica tried her best to get away from the robot, but she needed to move faster. She came up with a plan!

Looking around her, she spotted a couple of convertible cars. She hurriedly slipped her feet into them and skated onto the Golden Gate Bridge.

The alien continued chasing Ginormica and crashed right into the side of the bridge, tearing through the metal structure and sending cars and trucks flying.

"No, no, get away from me," yelled Ginormica. She fought as hard as she could to escape the clutches of the giant robot alien, but he was fast catching up on her.

Just as the robot was about to grab Ginormica, Insectosaurus stepped in. He had spotted she was in trouble and quickly shot silk fibres into the robot's eye, momentarily blinding him and giving Ginormica just enough time to run away.

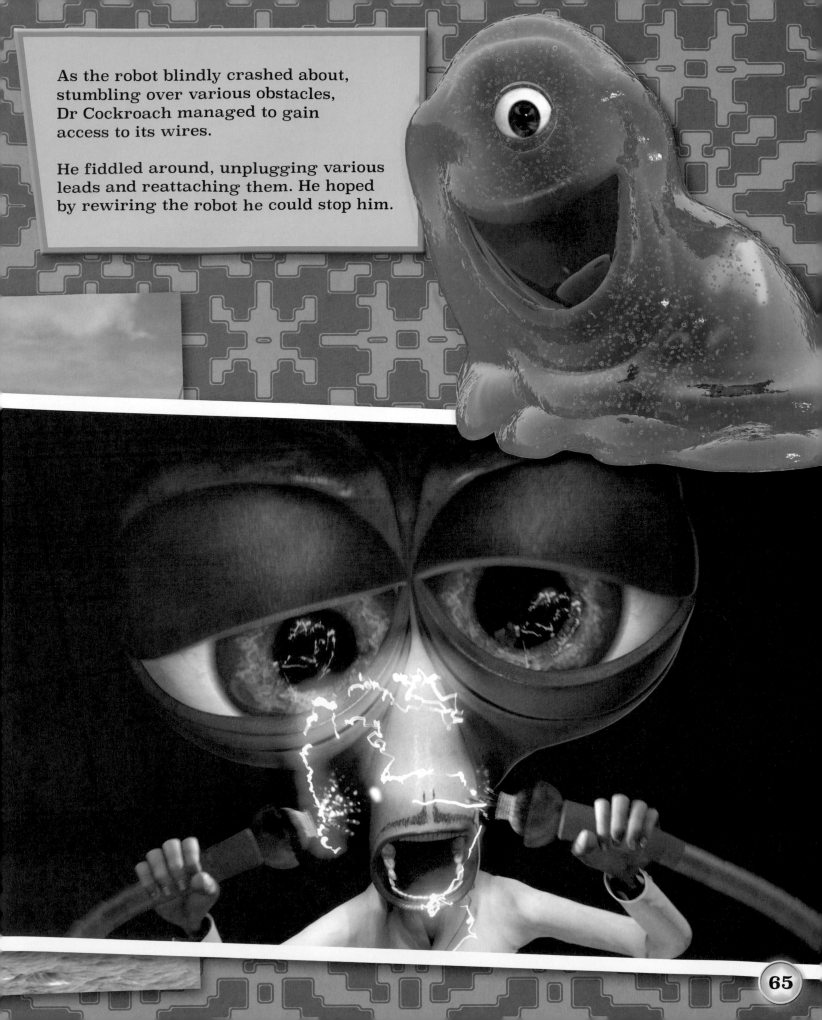

As the robot blindly crashed about, stumbling over various obstacles, Dr Cockroach managed to gain access to its wires.

He fiddled around, unplugging various leads and reattaching them. He hoped by rewiring the robot he could stop him.

Ginormica knew it was up to her to stop the robot. She grabbed a fistful of loose wires, which were hanging from the bridge.

Taking advantage of the robot's blindness and slowing pace, she wound the wires round his huge arms.
"I've got this!" she cried.

The robot went crashing to the ground, where the rest of the bridge fell onto him, stopping him for good.

The battle was over. For a moment, the team of monsters were too stunned to speak and then they realised that they had done it. They had rescued the people of America and were no longer monsters. They were heroes.

KUNG FU PANDA

DREAMWORKS

Legend tells of a kung fu warrior who travels the land, protecting the innocent and leaving his enemies blind with his awesomeness. Even the greatest warriors bow to... the Dragon Warrior.

In the Valley of Peace, silence was interrupted by a loud snore. "Po! Get up! You'll be late for work!" Po's father yelled. Po was a dreamer. He longed to become a hero as great and brave as the Dragon Warrior. Po rushed downstairs to his father's crowded noodle shop and began work.

Meanwhile, at the Jade Palace, legendary kung fu teacher Master Shifu was training the Furious Five, an elite kung fu team, when Master Oogway interrupted. "I've had a vision," Oogway said. "Tai Lung will return."

Tai Lung, once a promising pupil of Shifu, had been imprisoned after he tried to steal the Dragon Scroll and its secret to unlimited power.

Shifu was concerned because Oogway's visions were never wrong. They had to choose a new Dragon Warrior and they quickly headed to the arena.

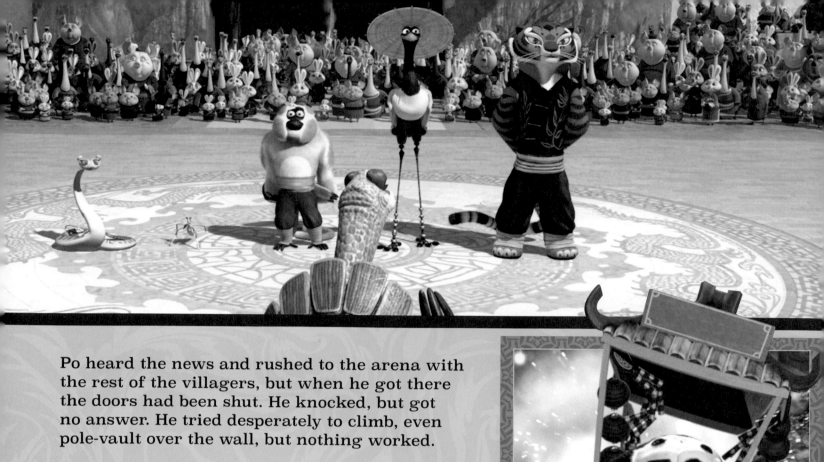

Po heard the news and rushed to the arena with the rest of the villagers, but when he got there the doors had been shut. He knocked, but got no answer. He tried desperately to climb, even pole-vault over the wall, but nothing worked.

Suddenly, Po had an idea. He strapped himself to a fireworks cart and launched himself into the arena, landing in front of a surprised Master Oogway.

"The universe has brought us the Dragon Warrior," Oogway declared, pointing at Po. Shifu couldn't believe it. This panda was no Dragon Warrior!

Soon, Po found himself in the Sacred Hall of Heroes. It was the coolest place he had ever seen, with awesome kung fu artefacts on show. Po ran around looking at them all.

"Turn around," said a voice from behind Po.

"Master Shifu!" Po cried.

As Po turned, he bumped into an urn, sending it crashing to the floor. Shifu wasn't impressed with this clumsy, so-called Dragon Warrior. He decided to test Po with the Wuxi Finger Hold. It really hurt, but Po still thought it was pretty cool.

Po followed Shifu to the training hall where the Furious Five were practising. Po was thrilled to watch his heroes, Masters Tigress, Monkey, Crane, Viper and Mantis, perform death-defying stunts and kung fu skills through a gauntlet of devices.

"Your turn, panda," said Shifu. Po joined in and was immediately flung, beaten, spun, twirled and thrown, landing at the feet of the disapproving Furious Five.

Po was embarrassed. He didn't fit in with the Furious Five and knew that they didn't want him there. He felt like an imposter. It was clear that they thought he could never be the Dragon Warrior. "Maybe I should quit and go back to making noodles," Po sighed.

Master Oogway overheard the panda's sad words and gave him some advice. "Yesterday is history, tomorrow is a mystery, but today is a gift. That is why it is the present." Po smiled. He was willing to try again.

Meanwhile, far away from the Jade Palace stood Tai Lung, surrounded by a thousand guards and locked in an impenetrable prison. He had waited years for his chance to escape. The time was now and he was ready.

The guards didn't stand a chance against his powerful kung fu moves. Dodging spears and arrows, he clawed his way up the rocky walls and swung himself to freedom.
At last, now he could return to the palace and claim his rightful title of Dragon Warrior!

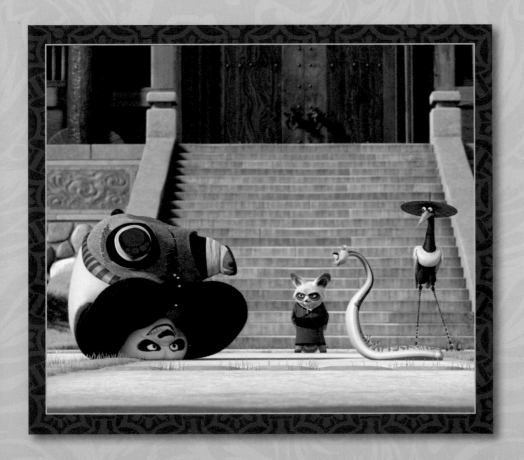

Back at the palace, Po was training hard. First, Viper flipped him ears over heels, sending him crashing down onto his head.

"That was awesome!" Po cried.

Next was Monkey. He whacked Po all over his body with a bamboo cane. Then, it was Shifu's turn.

"The path to victory is to use your opponent's strength against him until he fails or quits," he said wisely, grabbing Po in a powerful kung fu hold.

Po was inspired. "Don't worry, Master Shifu. I'll never quit!"

Soon, the news about Tai Lung's escape reached the palace. Time was running out for Po to master kung fu! Shifu rushed to tell Oogway.

"That is bad news," Oogway said. "If you do not believe that the Dragon Warrior can stop him."

"Master, that panda is not the Dragon Warrior!" Shifu cried.

"You just need to believe, Shifu," Oogway told him. "Now, you must continue without me."

He handed his staff to Shifu and disappeared forever in a swirl of petals.

At the bunkhouse, Shifu found Po goofing off with the Furious Five.
"Tai Lung is coming," said Shifu. "Po, you're the only one who can stop him."
"What?" laughed Po, nervously. "I'm going to stop Tai Lung?"

As Shifu turned to speak to the Furious Five, Po dashed for the door and ran.
He was scared of facing Tai Lung.
"Po, I can train you," said Shifu when he caught up to Po. "I will turn you into
the Dragon Warrior. Have faith in your ability."

Tigress didn't agree with Shifu's faith in Po and decided to face Tai Lung by herself.

As she sneaked out, the others chased after her. "Don't try and stop me," warned Tigress. "We won't," Viper said. "We want to help!"

The Furious Five headed out and soon found Tai Lung on a rope bridge spanning a vast gorge. They began their attack, but the snow leopard overpowered the group using a special kung fu nerve attack to freeze them in place. Tai Lung snarled and bounded away towards the valley.

Back at the palace, Shifu was trying to work out how to motivate Po to train. As he watched the panda eat and eat and eat, he understood. This was the key to the panda's greatness!

Shifu changed his training plans for Po. Instead of the usual kung fu methods, Master Shifu used stir-fry and dumplings to build and refine Po's skills. It worked! Po got better and better.

Po's dreams were coming true. Maybe he was worthy of being the Dragon Warrior after all!

The Furious Five returned and told Shifu of their battle with Tai Lung. Shifu decided that Po needed to meet his destiny head-on and gave him the Dragon Scroll.

"Read it," he said. "It will help you to become the Dragon Warrior."

Po unrolled the scroll and gasped. "It's blank!"

All his new confidence disappeared. Tai Lung had already defeated the Furious Five. How was a panda like Po ever supposed to beat him? Even Shifu didn't understand the meaning of the blank scroll, but he knew he must evacuate the palace before Tai Lung arrived.

Po walked sadly towards his father's noodle shop. Seeing that his son was upset, Po's father decided it was time to trust him with the secret ingredient in his noodle soup.

"There is no secret ingredient," he told Po. "To make something special, you just have to believe it's special."

Po was shocked. "There is no secret ingredient?" He unrolled the blank scroll again and saw his reflection in the shiny surface. It all made sense, there was no secret of the scroll.

Now Po understood what he had to do!

When Tai Lung arrived at the palace, Shifu was waiting.
"I am home, Master," Tai Lung said.
"This is no longer your home," Shifu replied. "You dishonoured me. I am no longer your master."

The two warriors began a fierce fight, but Shifu was soon overpowered by Tai Lung's strength.

Po burst in just as Tai Lung was about to make a deadly move. Tai Lung couldn't believe that a panda was the Dragon Warrior. "What are you going to do, big guy?" he taunted. "Sit on me?"

Po began to fight, but he didn't use the same kung fu moves as other warriors... he had his own unique, panda style. The battle raged down the palace steps and into the village.

Po battled fiercely and, in one incredible move, bounced Tai Lung off his belly and up into the air. When the dust settled, Po jumped up and snatched Tai Lung's finger.

"Not the Wuxi Finger Hold!" yelled Tai Lung. The panda flexed his pinkie and it was all over.

Po had won!

Cheers rang out from every direction as Po marched victoriously
through the Valley. Po's father looked on at his son, proudly.

Shifu could hardly believe it.
"It is as Oogway foretold," he said. "You truly are the Dragon
Warrior. Thank you, Po!"
The Furious Five faced Po, smiled and then bowed with respect.

Po started to smile, too. It was great that everyone finally believed
he was the Dragon Warrior, but it was even better believing
in himself!

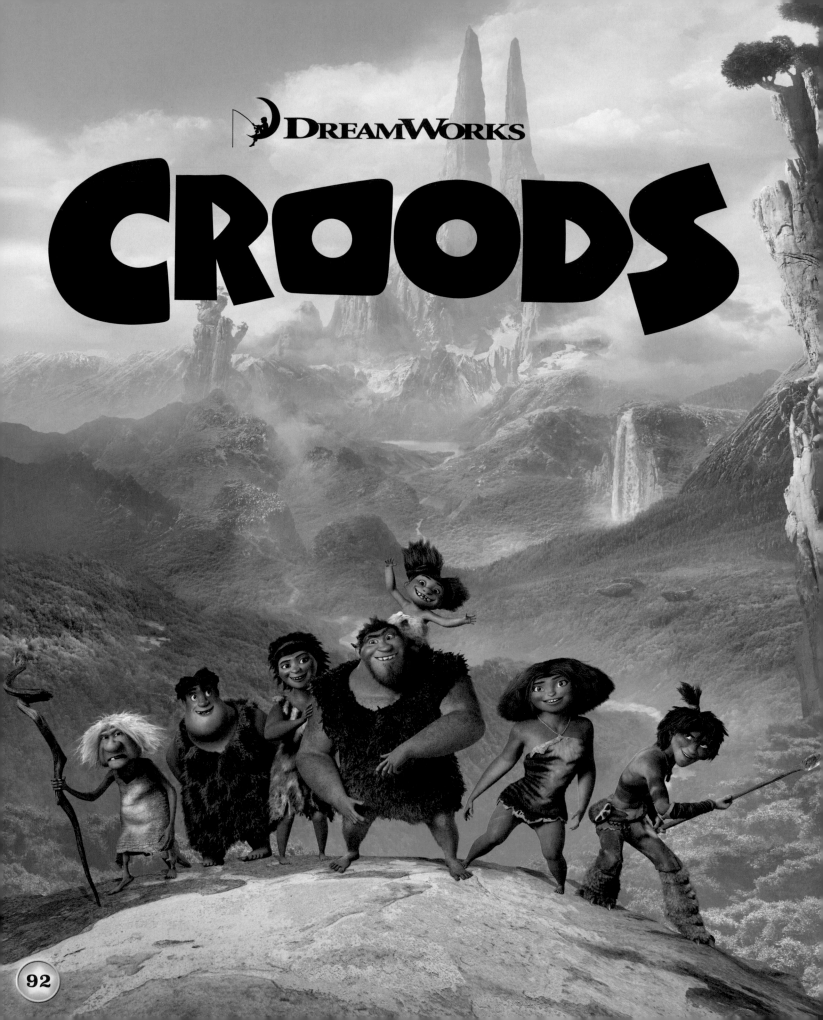

Meet the Croods – Grug, his wife, Ugga and their children, Eep, Thunk and Sandy, as well as Grug's mother-in-law, Gran. The Croods spend most of their days in their cave, hidden safely away from the harsh outside world. For fun, Grug tells stories and draws on the cave walls and every night the entire family sleep in a large pile to stay warm and comfy.

Big, brave and strong, Grug is the leader of the Croods family. His job is to protect and provide for them. He constantly reminds everyone to "never, not be afraid." After all, the outside world is filled with dangerous animals. Bear Owls are creatures with the strength of a bear and an owl's night vision. Liyotes have lizard-like faces and coyote-like speed and Trip Gerbils look adorable, but will gladly knock you down to steal your food. The Croods only leave the cave for one reason...

... to find food!

One night, Grug's daughter, Eep, sneaked out
of the family's cave to explore.
A mysterious light led her to a strange animal.
Eep grabbed the creature and threw it to
the ground.
The creature suddenly pulled off a mask.
It was a boy!
"Ow!" the boy yelled.
Eep was surprised.
"You talk!" she said.
"I'm a person, like you," he answered.
Eep lifted the boy off the ground with one hand.
"Well... sort of like you," the boy said, smiling.

The boy introduced himself as Guy and his pet, Belt. Guy told Eep he could make the sun come out whenever he liked. He called it 'fire'. Guy explained he often used fire to protect himself.

Eep was amazed and grabbed Guy. She shook him, trying to make more fire. "It doesn't come out of me!" Guy said, grinning.

Guy gave Eep a shell and told her that if she ever found herself in danger, she could call him with the shell and he would come.

The next morning, Eep told her family about Guy, the strange light called fire and his offer of help. Grug was furious with his daughter for taking such a risk.
"New is a big problem," he told Eep. "New is always bad!"

Suddenly, the ground began to shake. It was a huge earthquake. Grug grabbed his family and together they huddled in a tight ball until the ground eventually stopped shaking.

Once it was safe, the Croods looked around. Their cave had been completely destroyed. As they stood, wondering what to do next, a Bear Owl chased them off a cliff. The Croods had no choice, but to venture into the world that they were so afraid of.

Grug and his family quickly made their way into a jungle.

Suddenly, from nowhere, they were surrounded by a pack of Punch Monkeys.
"I'll take care of this," Grug said, launching into his trademark threat display.

The Punch Monkeys laughed and took it in turns to punch Grug in the face.
They thought that it was lots of fun.
"Go get 'em, Dad!" Thunk cheered, but as the Punch Monkeys continued to
beat up Grug, Thunk made a suggestion to help him.
"Dad, I've got it! Just stop running into their fists."

Eventually, Grug fought the Punch Monkeys away and the Croods were able to continue with their dangerous journey.

Soon, they stumbled across a new cave, which they thought would keep them safe.

As they stepped inside, the entrance slammed shut and everything went very dark. Suddenly, Thunk cried, "Hey, this cave has a tongue."

The Croods had run straight into the mouth of a Land Whale.

Luckily, the whale didn't think the Croods tasted very nice and shot them out through its blowhole and up into the air.

As the Croods scrambled to safety, a swarm of Piranhakeets appeared and gobbled up the entire Land Whale in a matter of seconds. As the Piranhakeets continued with their Land Whale feast, Eep started to worry that her family would be the next treat, so she decided it was time to call Guy for help. She took the shell from her belt and blew it. The noise echoed through the valley around them.

In the distance, Guy heard the sound. Knowing his friend, Eep, was in trouble, he ran as fast as he could towards it.

As he got closer, he struck a spark with two stones, setting light to a torch, that flared up into roaring flames. He waved it at the Piranhakeets who all scattered away, leaving the Croods safe, but shocked.

The Croods thanked Guy, but were more fascinated
by the fire he held. It was new and mysterious to them.

As they began to investigate, embers fell onto Thunk's tunic,
causing it to burst into flames.
"It likes me!" he said. "Hey! It's biting me! Ow! Stop!" he shouted.

Then, Gran realised her walking stick was on fire, too.
She slammed the stick down to put out the fire, but that
only helped start lots more smaller fires.

Gran furiously banged her stick on the ground until the flames died down. What she didn't realise was that a tiny spark had flown from her stick into a nearby cornfield.

Soon, ears of corn soared into the sky and exploded into popcorn like colourful and tasty fireworks.

Despite Guy helping them, Grug still didn't trust him. Grug didn't like anything that was different. Guy sensed Grug's distrust.

Grug ordered Guy to stay with the family until they found a new home, so Guy suggested they should head towards the high mountains. Grug thought he should be the one making decisions for his family, so he disagreed with the plan. Then, Guy explained that the high mountains were full of large caves. Grug desperately wanted to find his family a safe, new home, so he changed his mind. The rest of the family weren't so sure about the trip, but Grug convinced them.

"We'll tell stories. We'll laugh. We'll become closer as a family," said Grug.

The family and Guy set off, but before long, the Croods became grouchy and hungry on their road trip. Thunk saw a Turkeyfish and tried to catch it, but tripped and fell on a Brontoscorpion, so the humongous insect became dinner instead. "Eat up before it stops wriggling," Grug told everyone.

Watching the Croods eat the disgusting insect made Guy feel sick, especially when it kept wriggling and moving around. "Food fixes everything!" Grug said to Guy.

Guy leaned over to Eep
and told her that he was
hungry, too.
"You can have some bug
for dinner," Eep said, smiling.
"There's plenty of bug!"

Guy explained that he didn't
want to eat bug and showed
Eep how to set up a trap to
catch the Turkeyfish.

Finally, after a short wait, the Turkeyfish was caught in the trap. Guy showed Eep how to roast it over a fire. The Croods had never tasted anything so delicious, or anything cooked before.
"It's an avalanche of flavour," cried Thunk.
"Looks like we won't have any leftovers," said Guy, as he watched the Croods eat every last piece of the delicious roasted bird.

Eep asked what a leftover was.
"It's when you have so much food to eat you have some left over," Guy explained.
"That never happens to us!" Eep declared. "We eat everything we catch."

The family finished their feast and continued on their journey.

Soon, they came to a brightly coloured field of coral. With each step they took, the jagged coral cut at their bare feet. Guy was wearing boots and walked across the coral with ease.

Thunk, who had been experimenting with new ways to walk over the coral, shouted out suggestions to everyone.
"Jumping on the rocks does not help. Do not walk on your hands, the hands do not help at all!"

Guy felt bad for the family and decided to help them by making everyone shoes out of leaves and fish. He quickly began and soon had a pair for each member of the family.

After slipping on his fishy shoes, Thunk looked down and was amazed to see the fish blinking back at him!
"Aaaah!" he screamed. Thunk wasn't sure that he liked his squelchy new shoes.

Once safely over the coral, the Croods and Guy continued with their journey, getting closer and closer to the huge mountains.

Soon, with the mountains only a short distance away, the Croods found their path blocked by a maze with many different entrances.

Guy suggested they split up and each take a different route, but Grug was horrified by the idea. "Croods stick together," he said, sternly.

Suddenly, the ground shook and fell away beneath the Croods' feet. When the dust eventually settled, they realised they had been separated from each other after all.

At first, the Croods were scared to be on their own, but as they became used to their surroundings, they started to have fun and enjoy themselves.

Thunk played catch with a Crocopup, while Eep discovered a flower Guy had left on her path. Even Gran and Ugga had fun camouflaging themselves as flowers to fool meat-eating plants. Grug was the only one not having fun. He couldn't find his way out of the maze and reluctantly blew on a shell to call for help.

After finding their separate ways out of the maze, the Croods found they had made it to the base of the mountains.

Just then, the ground rumbled once more. It was another earthquake. The family stood by, as they watched the ground before them open up creating a huge gap between them and the mountains. No one knew what to do.

Grug paused for a moment and then, much to everyone's surprise, instructed the family to separate. Grug knew the only way to protect his family was to get them to the other side of the chasm using his strength.

Grug explained that he would throw each of them across the chasm.

Grug offered to throw Guy across first. Grug knew that his family would be safe with Guy on the other side. Then, one-by-one, Grug powerfully, yet carefully, threw each member of his family to the other side of the gap.

His family were finally safe, but Grug was still trapped with no one to throw him across.

Later, as Grug was trapped in a cave, he thought about his family and their strange new friend. Grug realised that he had been wrong all along. Bravery wasn't about hiding and cowering away from problems, bravery was about trying new things and overcoming problems. Grug decided if he was going to save himself then he had to do something new and fast. He looked around to see what he could use and quickly gathered some things.

Within moments, Grug had built himself a flying machine!

Grug took a leap of faith and flew off the edge of the gap. He sailed over the chasm and into the open arms of his waiting family. The Croods were back together and ready to explore a beautiful new world together!

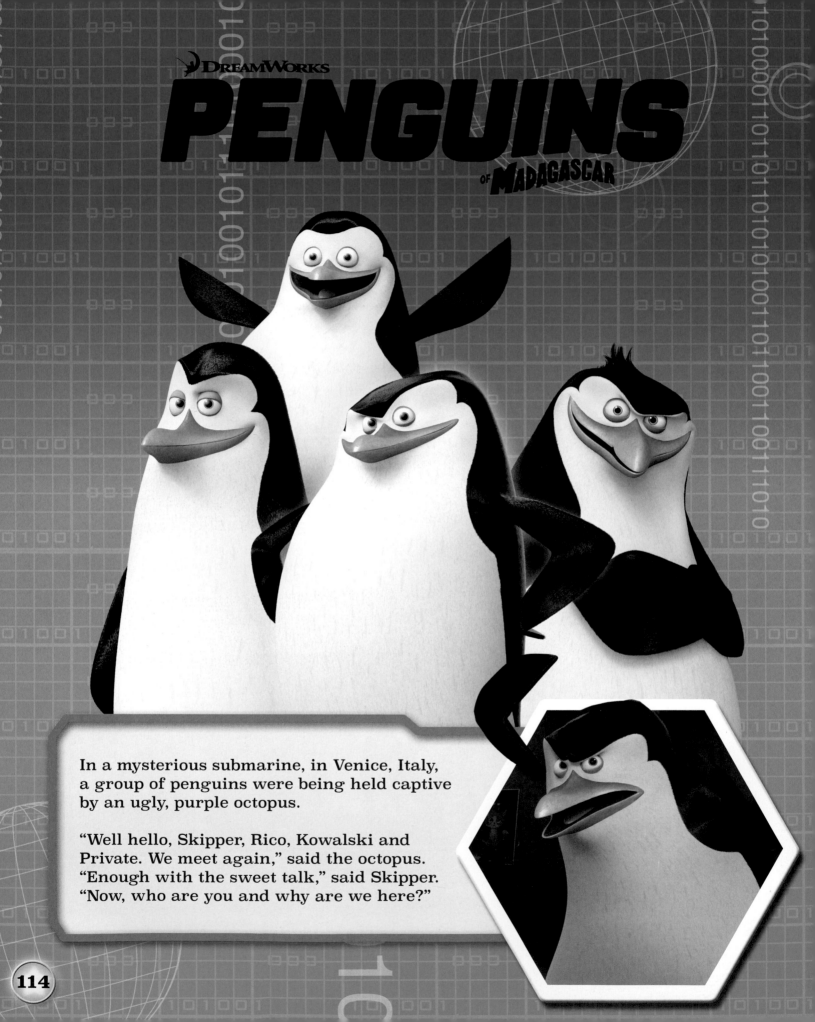

DREAMWORKS
PENGUINS
OF MADAGASCAR

In a mysterious submarine, in Venice, Italy, a group of penguins were being held captive by an ugly, purple octopus.

"Well hello, Skipper, Rico, Kowalski and Private. We meet again," said the octopus. "Enough with the sweet talk," said Skipper. "Now, who are you and why are we here?"

The octopus smiled.

"I... am... DAVE!" he cried. "Soon after I started life in my first aquarium, people ignored me. It was always about the cute penguins. Well not for long! I have developed a serum-firing ray machine to take away your cuteness. Soon, penguins around the world will be hideous and then people will love me."

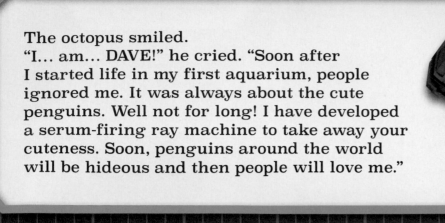

"Not on my watch, Derek," said Skipper. The penguins wriggled free and leapt into action. In the struggle, Dave lost his grip on the serum bottle he was holding.
"Dave!" cried the octopus. "My name is Dave!"
The serum flew through the air. Rico slid to catch it, but one of Dave's tentacles caught it first.

Suddenly, octopus henchmen burst in and charged at the penguins.

"Kowalski, escape route!" shouted Skipper. The penguins leapt through a hatch in the roof and found themselves on a canal. "Alright boys, just like Cuba," said Skipper.

The penguins leapt off the submarine and landed in a passing gondola. Just then, a swarm of octopus henchmen scrambled out of the submarine and chased them.

The four penguins paddled quickly and sped across the water, dodging obstacles as they rushed to get away.

"Sir, octopuses at twelve o'clock," said Kowalski.

"Good, it's only quarter past ten," replied Skipper.

As the penguins rowed away, the octopus henchmen used two lamp posts as a slingshot and propelled themselves onto the penguins' gondola.

As Skipper moved into battle stance, the boat zoomed under a washing line and a sock covered his face.
"I've lost visual!" he cried. "Kowalski, be my eyes." Skipper swung an oar wildly, hitting one, then two octopus henchmen.

Suddenly, the boat hit a wall and the penguins were thrown through the air. After a wild chase on land, they ended up in an alley with no exit. The octopus henchmen had them surrounded.

"Okay boys, now we spring our trap,"
said Skipper, confidently.
"I'm not so sure that they're the ones that
are trapped, sir," said Kowalski.

Suddenly, an owl swooped down and carried off
one of the henchmen. Then, a baby seal jumped in and took out another, before a
polar bear appeared and zapped the last octopus with a laser. The penguins had
no idea what was happening.

The polar bear, owl and seal all stood in front of the surprised penguins, as a jet soared overhead. From it, a wolf dropped to the ground.
"Don't panic penguins. You are now under the protection of the North Wind," said the wolf. "My name is classified and this is my team. That armoured polar bear is Corporal. The lovely owl is Eva and finally, our explosives expert, Short Fuse. Come along, team, to the jet."

Reluctantly, the penguins followed the North Wind onto their jet.
"We have been after Dave for a while now," said Agent Classified, "but we have never been able to get close to him. Tell us what you know."
"We know that he's a whole heap of crazy," said Skipper. "We also know that you and your friends here ruined our trap to catch him."

Agent Classified laughed.
"Trap. What trap?" he said. "You were the ones who were trapped."

Skipper puffed out his chest. "Listen up, hot dog. We had things under control," he said.

Agent Classified sniggered, while Corporal just stared at the cute penguins. "We are the elite-est of the elite," boasted Skipper. "The cream of the crop and we don't need you, or your fancy flying machine!"

Agent Classified reached down beside him as Skipper kept talking.

"Okay, boys. This is the mission we've been preparing for our entire lives. Penguins are planning this party."

Suddenly, there was a sound, as Agent Classified fired his sleep darts into the four penguins. He smiled, as the four penguins drifted off quietly to sleep.

The penguins awoke to find themselves in the cargo hold of the jet.

"Sir, we're five miles up. Our options are limited," said Kowalski, scanning the area. "I make my own options," replied Skipper hitting a big, red button with his flipper. An alarm sounded and the cargo doors opened. The penguins and all the North Wind's cargo boxes tumbled out!

The penguins fell through the air, skilfully bouncing from cargo box to cargo box, trying to find something to help them.

Suddenly, they found a bouncy castle. Using Rico like a pump, they inflated it just in time and bounced off, landing safely in a desert.
"Right, boys, next stop, civilization to take down Dave," said Skipper, leading the way.

Eventually, the penguins reached the home of the famous Mermaid Penguins at the aquarium in Shanghai, Dave's final target. "Sir, looks like Dave hasn't been here yet. We still have time to stop him," reported Kowalski.
"Now, all we need is a man on the inside," said Skipper, looking at Private.

Later that evening, the trap was set. Private was dressed as a Mermaid Penguin while Skipper, Kowalski and Rico waited for Dave. They didn't have long to wait. Soon, Dave appeared and Skipper raced after him.

Suddenly, the North Wind were there, too. Agent Classified and Skipper began to argue over who would bring Dave to justice. Meanwhile, Dave escaped and he took Private with him!

"Private!" cried Skipper, running after Dave. Skipper, Kowalski and Rico got outside just in time to see Dave's submarine disappear under the water. Skipper looked around and saw the North Wind's jet and the three penguins jumped inside.

The North Wind were close behind and saw their jet being taken. "Quick, into this boat!" cried Agent Classified.

Aboard the jet, Skipper was frantically pressing buttons and twisting dials. "Kowalski, how do you steer this thing!" he cried.
"I'm afraid I don't know, sir," replied Kowalski. "We're penguins, we're not supposed to fly."

The jet quickly began to spin out of control and crashed into Agent Classified's boat, leaving the penguins and the North Wind stranded at sea. Together, they slowly followed Dave's course towards his secret island.

As night fell, the two teams located Dave's evil lair and stealthily snuck inside. Just as they were about to take down Dave, an alarm sounded and the room was filled with octopus henchmen.

The penguins and the North Wind were captured. Elsewhere, Private had managed to escape. It was up to him to save his friends and penguin-kind.

Private searched all over the island and soon found his friends and the North Wind locked in a cage. He quickly unlocked it and opened the door.

"Boys, it's time to take care of these slimy sea-dwellers," said Skipper. The team made their way to Dave's ray machine and jumped into action, bravely fighting the henchmen. Soon, the only octopus left was Dave.

SLAP!

CRACK!

POW!

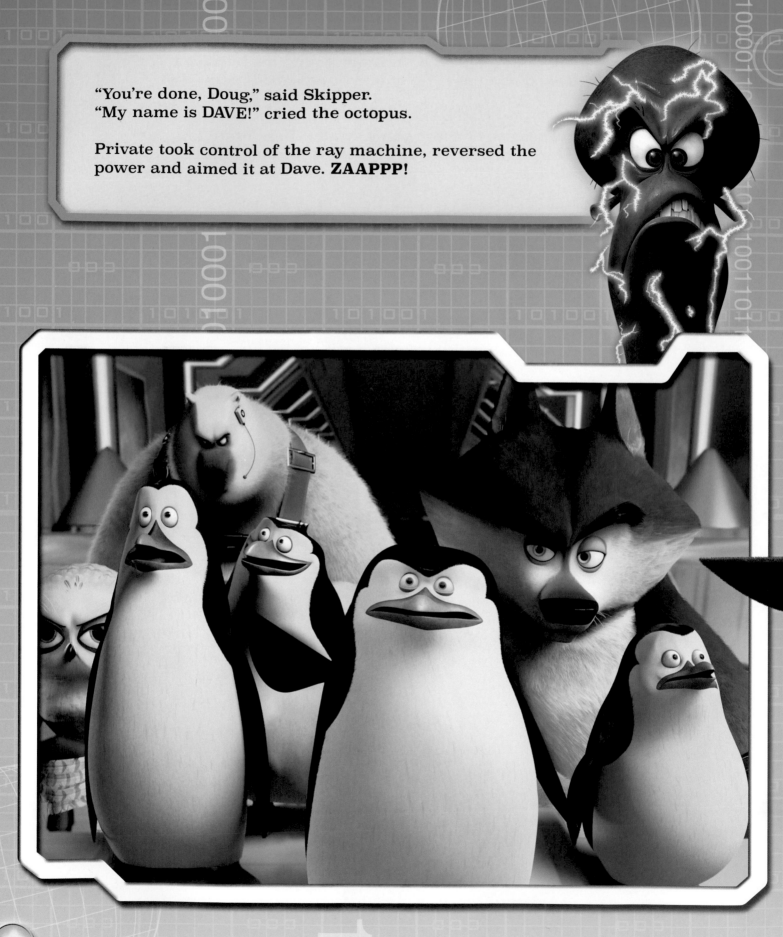

"You're done, Doug," said Skipper.
"My name is DAVE!" cried the octopus.

Private took control of the ray machine, reversed the power and aimed it at Dave. **ZAAPPP!**

Dave had been defeated and the cuteness of all penguin-kind was secured at last.

"Well done, boys, especially you, Private. That's another plan that worked perfectly," said Skipper, smiling.

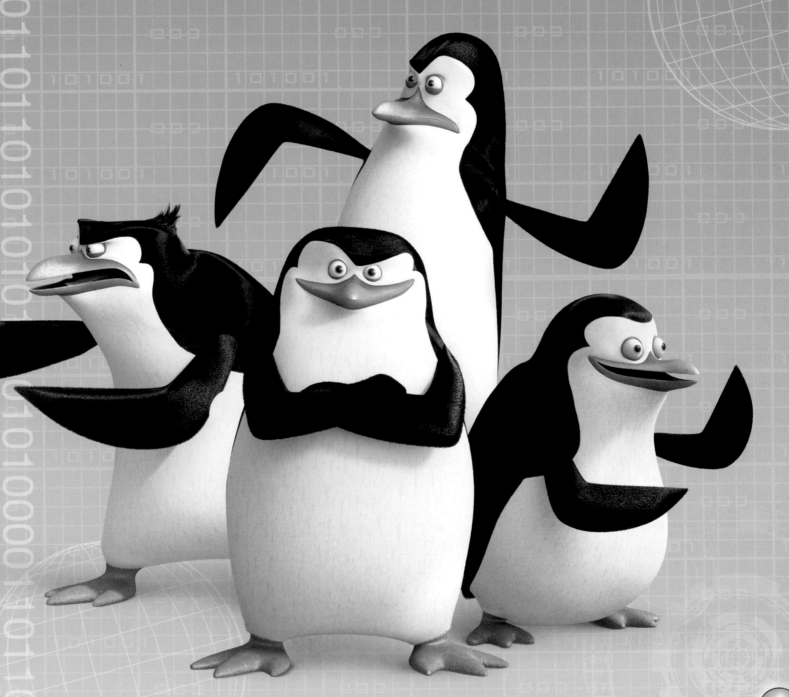

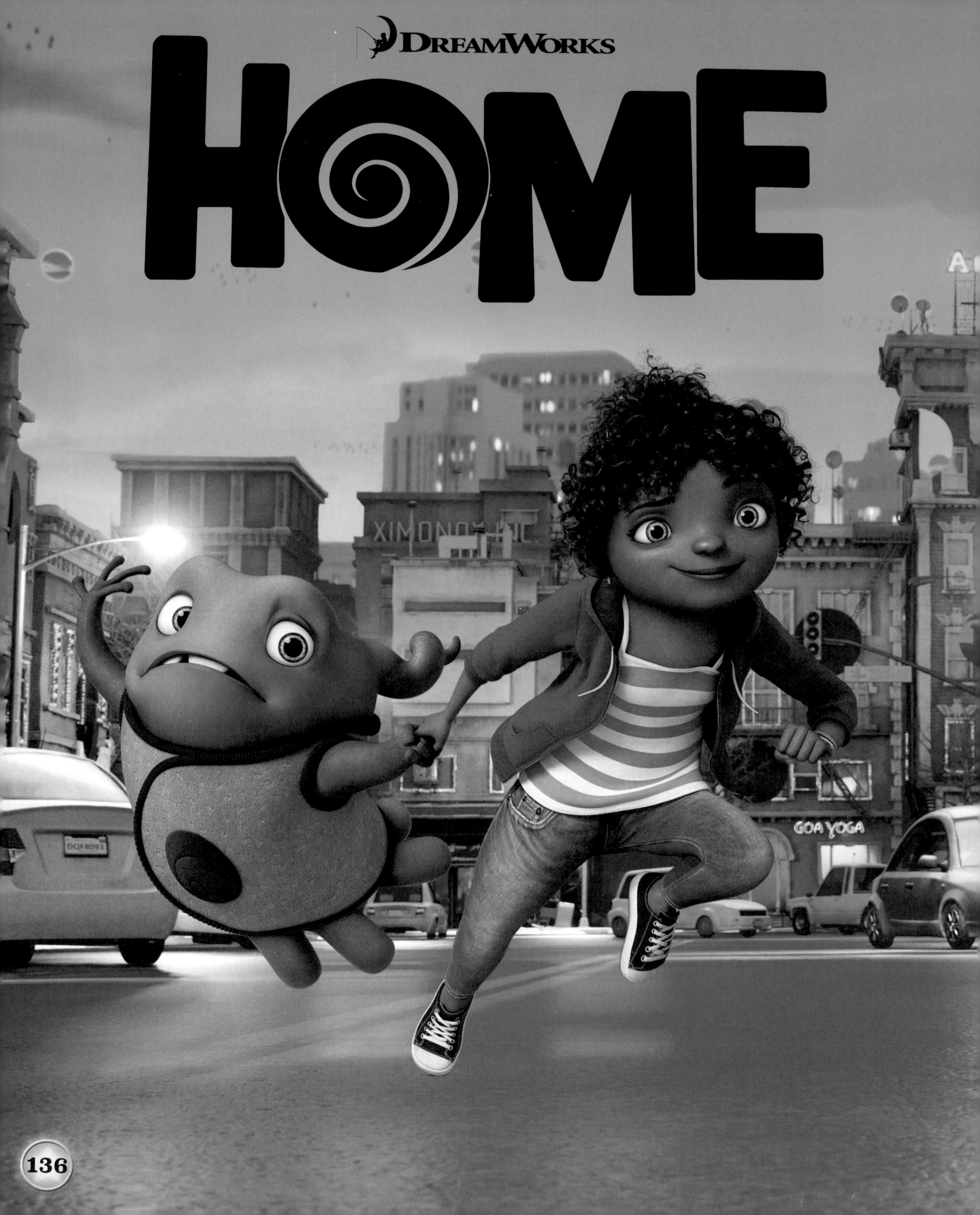
DreamWorks
HOME
GOA YOGA

In the deepest, darkest depths of the galaxy, Captain Smek, the leader of an alien race called the Boov, was running away.

"Retreat to the ship, fellow Boov!" he cried, as a shadowy figure chased after him. Captain Smek dived through the doorway of his ship, just as the shadow loomed closer.

"Take off!" he shouted, panicking.

As the ship hurtled through the sky towards the stars, Captain Smek realised that he was holding something in his hand, a long staff with what looked like a stone on top. Puzzled, he looked at the staff and shrugged. "It is too late to return it now," he said, obviously too scared to turn the ship around. As he spoke, a small Boov began to speak. "Shhh!" said Captain Smek, tapping the small Boov on the head with the stone-tipped staff. Captain Smek thought for a moment and then declared, "From this day forward, this staff shall be known as the Shusher," he said, proudly.

The mysterious shadow, a member of the alien race known as the Gorg, watched the ship disappear into the distance and vowed to chase the Boov across the galaxy. Since that day, every planet that the Boov have tried to call home has come under attack and, ultimately, been destroyed by the Gorg.

YEARS LATER...

A tired-looking Captain Smek looked back at another burning planet they had just left behind, when suddenly, an alarm sounded. "Captain, we have found a suitable planet that the Gorg will never find," said a Big Brain Boov. "The computer registers it as being named Earth."

"Earth," said Captain Smek. "I like it. Plot a course to Earth. My fellow Boov, I have saved us once again!" The Boov ship powered up and, with a flash of light, sped towards the new and unfamiliar planet.

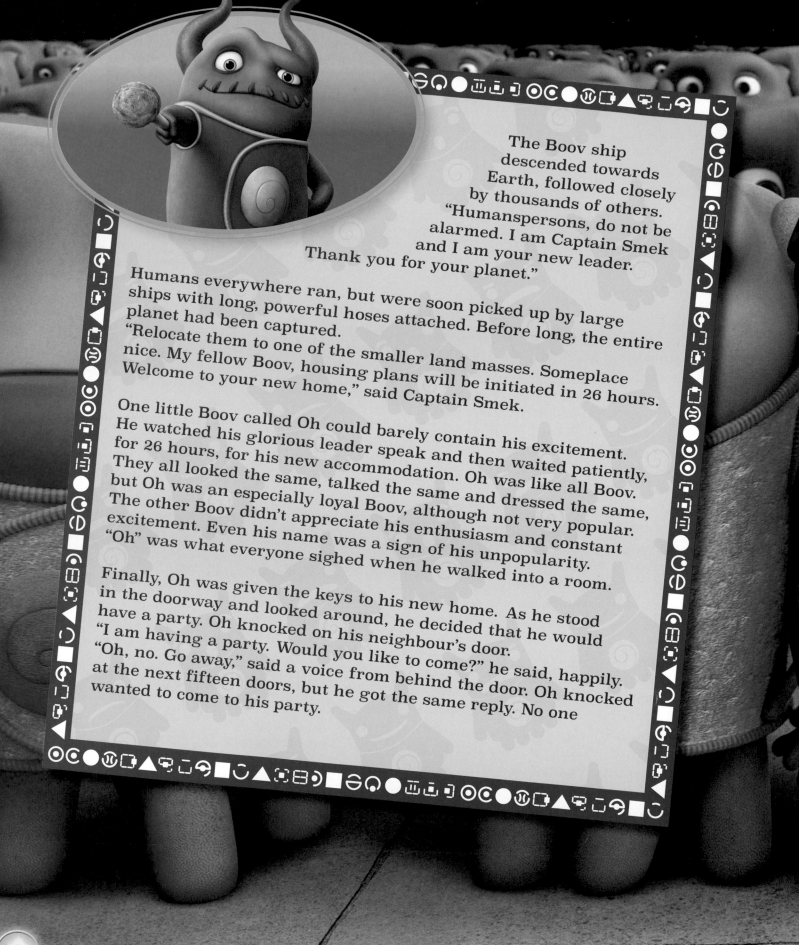

The Boov ship descended towards Earth, followed closely by thousands of others. "Humanspersons, do not be alarmed. I am Captain Smek and I am your new leader. Thank you for your planet."

Humans everywhere ran, but were soon picked up by large ships with long, powerful hoses attached. Before long, the entire planet had been captured. "Relocate them to one of the smaller land masses. Someplace nice. My fellow Boov, housing plans will be initiated in 26 hours. Welcome to your new home," said Captain Smek.

One little Boov called Oh could barely contain his excitement. He watched his glorious leader speak and then waited patiently, for 26 hours, for his new accommodation. Oh was like all Boov. They all looked the same, talked the same and dressed the same, but Oh was an especially loyal Boov, although not very popular. The other Boov didn't appreciate his enthusiasm and constant excitement. Even his name was a sign of his unpopularity. "Oh" was what everyone sighed when he walked into a room.

Finally, Oh was given the keys to his new home. As he stood in the doorway and looked around, he decided that he would have a party. Oh knocked on his neighbour's door. "I am having a party. Would you like to come?" he said, happily. "Oh, no. Go away," said a voice from behind the door. Oh knocked at the next fifteen doors, but he got the same reply. No one wanted to come to his party.

As Oh stood beside his window, he saw a fellow Boov that he knew, Kyle, a Boov Traffic Cop. An excited Oh reached for his Bubble-ship pad, activated it and floated down to the street below.

"Hello, Kyle," said Oh.
"Oh, it is you," said Kyle, looking a little cross and frustrated.
"Would you like to come to my party?" asked Oh.
"No, I am busy that day," said Kyle, turning away.
"I have not given you the time or date yet?" said Oh, a little confused.
"I do not want to come to your silly party," said Kyle, getting cross.
"Okay, I will put you down as a maybe," said Oh. "Here, let me email you the address." Oh typed into a small, handheld computer and pressed **SEND**. Kyle's computer started to beep. Before long, Boov all across the world had received Oh's message.
"Oh, you have sent your silly message to the entire universe!" cried Kyle.
"That is okay, the more the merrier," said Oh.
"No, the ENTIRE universe, including our most feared enemy, the Gorg!" shouted Kyle, crossly.

Oh realised what he had just done. Suddenly, he began to panic. He wondered what Captain Smek would say. He would be in trouble for certain. Oh's skin began to turn bright yellow. All Boov had the ability to change colour depending on their mood and Oh's mood was scared!

Before he knew what was happening, Oh was running as fast as his six legs could carry him.

Meanwhile, across town, a young girl named Gratuity Tucci was hiding. Since those weird, purple aliens had come, she hadn't seen her mum and was starting to get worried. Gratuity cuddled up to her pet cat, Pig.
"Well Pig, it's just you and me, boy," she said, looking at a tattered and torn picture of herself hugging her mum.

Just then, Gratuity heard a noise in the hallway outside, followed by voices. "Welcome to your new home, my fellow Boov," said the voice. The door handle on Gratuity's front door began to rattle.
"We have to move, Pig, now!" said Gratuity, grabbing her bag and climbing through her bedroom window and onto the fire escape. Gratuity ran down the stairs as fast as she could, with Pig following close behind. All around her, she could hear voices and strange noises.

With a set of keys rattling in her hand, she headed for the road and stopped at her mum's car. Gratuity was too young to drive, but this was an emergency. Gratuity sat inside, put the keys into the ignition and started the car. With Pig on the passenger seat, Gratuity revved the engine and the car sprang into life, taking off down the road, swaying from left to right.

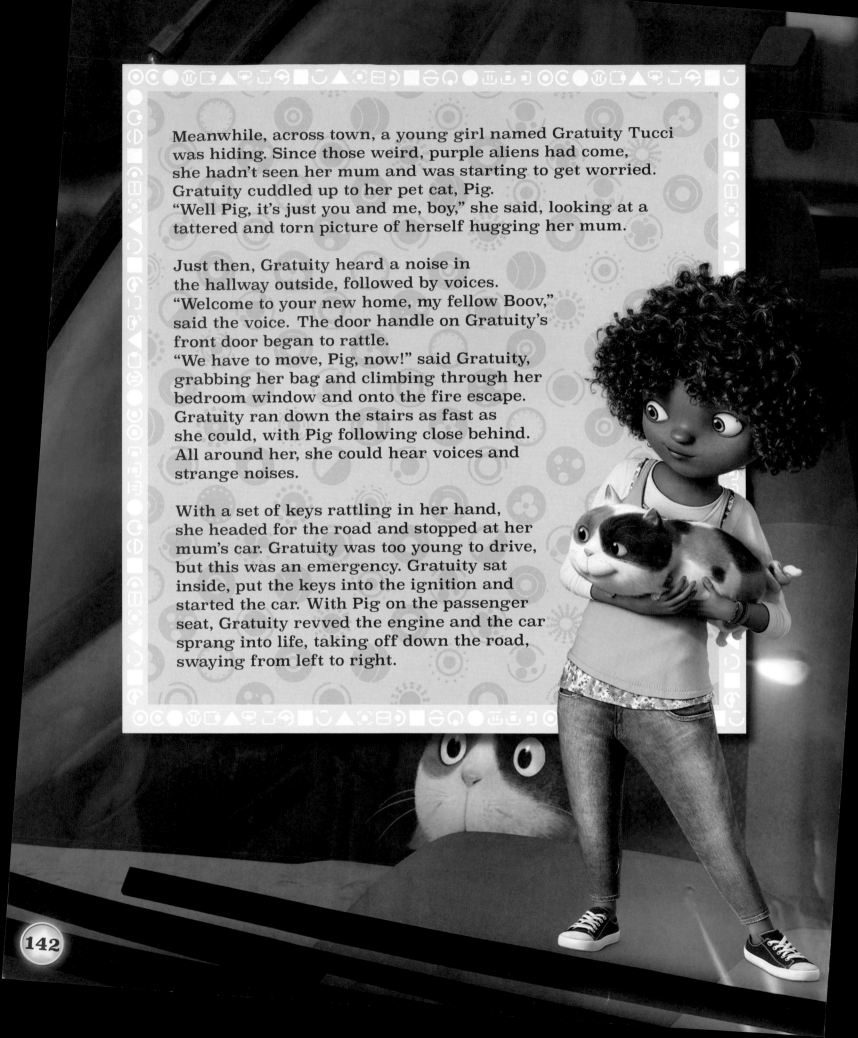

Gratuity struggled to control
her mum's car and soon found
herself heading straight for an
empty car park. The car crashed
into some bins and rolled to a stop.
Gratuity jumped out and rushed inside a nearby shop.
Closing the door behind her, she turned around and screamed.

Standing in front of her was Oh, drinking a can of motor oil.
Oh heard Gratuity scream, let out a screech and fell backwards
into a fridge. The door slammed shut after him.
"Let me out, or I will shoot forth the lasers from my eyeballs!"
he cried.
"You can do that?" asked Gratuity, curiously.
"Yeeesssss," said Oh.

Suddenly, Oh turned bright green and Gratuity guessed that
he wasn't telling the truth.
"See ya," she said, walking away.
"Wait!" cried Oh. "I saw you crash. If you free me, I can help
you to fix your car."
"Promise?" said Gratuity.
"Promise," said Oh, not really knowing what a promise was.
"I'm Gratuity. My friends call me Tip. I'm looking for my mum.
Can you help me to find her, too?" asked Tip, holding
the fridge handle.
"I promise," said Oh.

Tip opened the door and, using parts from the shop, Oh began
to fix Tip's car. Soon, it was a sparkling, shiny hover-car,
powered by three different types of slushy drink. They called
it Slushious.
"We need to go to Boov Central Command in Paris, Tip,"
said Oh. "They'll have information about where your mum is."
Tip smiled.
"Paris, here we come," she said.

At Boov Central Command, Captain Smek was panicking. "Ready my escape ship! Do not leave me alone! We are all doomed!" he cried, stamping all six feet on the ground. A Big Brain Boov stepped forward.

"Sir, could we not just try to stop the email from reaching the Gorg?"

"I've got it," said Captain Smek. "We could stop the email from reaching the Gorg!"

"Brilliant plan, Captain," said a small, scared-looking Boov. Captain Smek smiled.

"Once again, I, your brave leader, have saved us from certain extinction," he said.

A Big Brain Boov stepped forward and inputted the password for all Boov email, P-A-S-S-W-O-R-D. The screen flashed red – **ERROR**.

"What is happening?" said Captain Smek. "Why will it not work?"

"It appears that the fugitive, Oh, has changed his password, Captain," said the Big Brain Boov.

Captain Smek's arms flew up in the air. "Aaaaarrghggghhhh!! We are all doomed, erased, finished!"

The Boov stood and looked at each other awkwardly. "Erm, we could try to find the fugitive, Oh," said one Boov. Captain Smek heard this and stopped screaming. He turned away from the Boov, adjusted his top and then turned back around with a smile on his face.

"Find me the Boov who knows the fugitive the best," he said.

"It appears to be a Boov Traffic Cop named Kyle," said a Big Brain Boov, tapping away at a computer.

"Bring him to me," said Captain Smek.

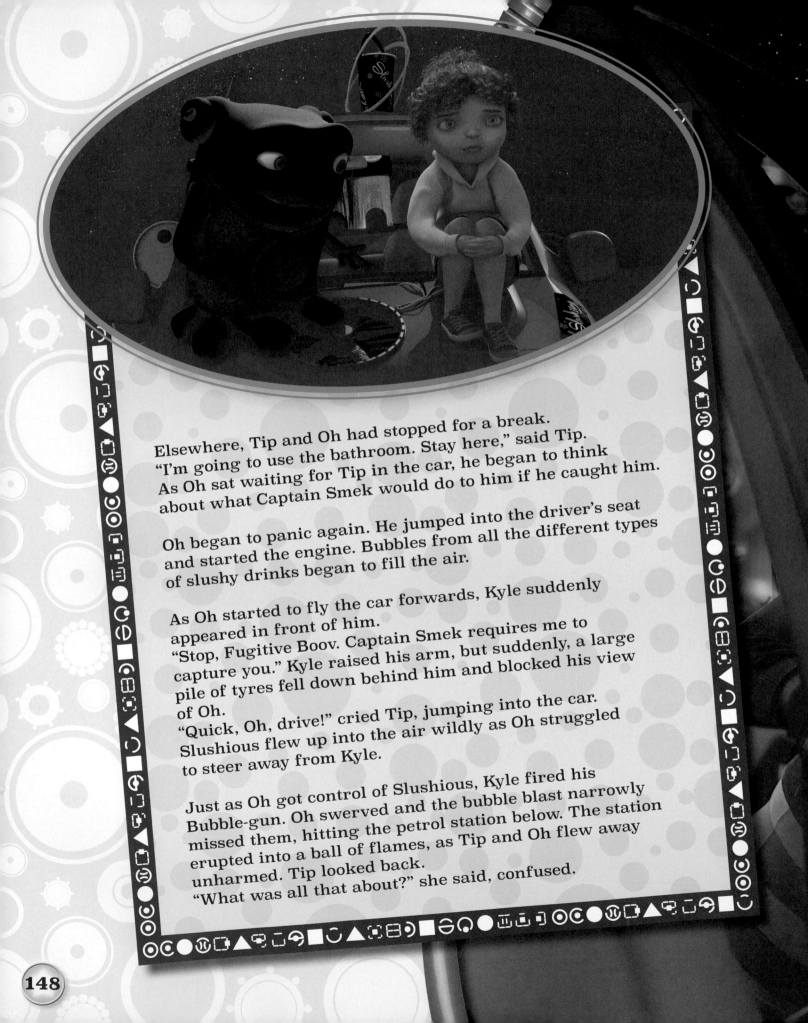

Elsewhere, Tip and Oh had stopped for a break.
"I'm going to use the bathroom. Stay here," said Tip.
As Oh sat waiting for Tip in the car, he began to think about what Captain Smek would do to him if he caught him.

Oh began to panic again. He jumped into the driver's seat and started the engine. Bubbles from all the different types of slushy drinks began to fill the air.

As Oh started to fly the car forwards, Kyle suddenly appeared in front of him.
"Stop, Fugitive Boov. Captain Smek requires me to capture you." Kyle raised his arm, but suddenly, a large pile of tyres fell down behind him and blocked his view of Oh.
"Quick, Oh, drive!" cried Tip, jumping into the car.
Slushious flew up into the air wildly as Oh struggled to steer away from Kyle.

Just as Oh got control of Slushious, Kyle fired his Bubble-gun. Oh swerved and the bubble blast narrowly missed them, hitting the petrol station below. The station erupted into a ball of flames, as Tip and Oh flew away unharmed. Tip looked back.
"What was all that about?" she said, confused.

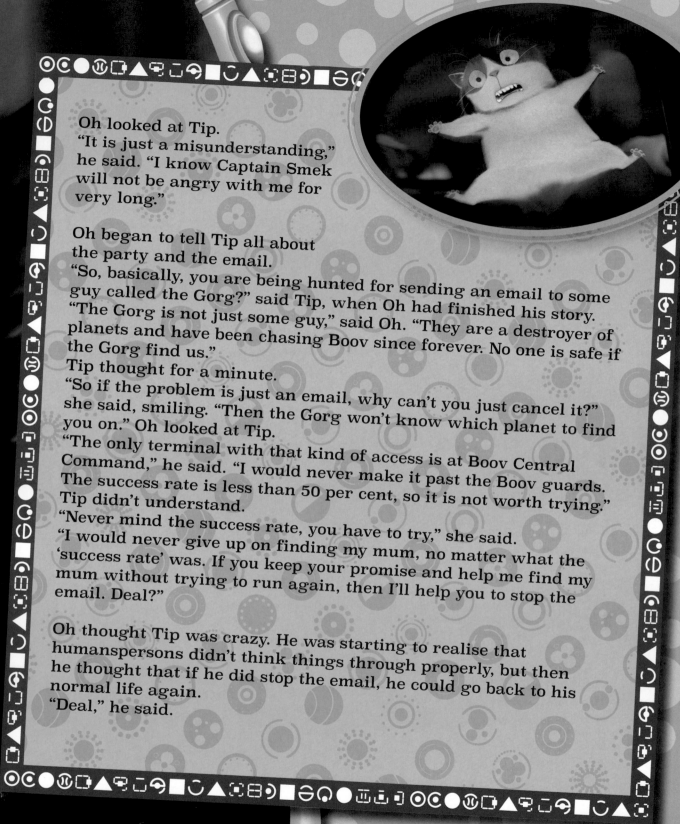

Oh looked at Tip.
"It is just a misunderstanding," he said. "I know Captain Smek will not be angry with me for very long."

Oh began to tell Tip all about the party and the email.
"So, basically, you are being hunted for sending an email to some guy called the Gorg?" said Tip, when Oh had finished his story.
"The Gorg is not just some guy," said Oh. "They are a destroyer of planets and have been chasing Boov since forever. No one is safe if the Gorg find us."
Tip thought for a minute.
"So if the problem is just an email, why can't you just cancel it?" she said, smiling. "Then the Gorg won't know which planet to find you on." Oh looked at Tip.
"The only terminal with that kind of access is at Boov Central Command," he said. "I would never make it past the Boov guards. The success rate is less than 50 per cent, so it is not worth trying."
Tip didn't understand.
"Never mind the success rate, you have to try," she said. "I would never give up on finding my mum, no matter what the 'success rate' was. If you keep your promise and help me find my mum without trying to run again, then I'll help you to stop the email. Deal?"

Oh thought Tip was crazy. He was starting to realise that humanspersons didn't think things through properly, but then he thought that if he did stop the email, he could go back to his normal life again.
"Deal," he said.

After a long flight, Oh and Tip reached Paris and parked Slushious somewhere out of the way.

"You stay here, Pig, this might be dangerous," said Tip, stroking the cat's fur as he slept. "So where is this Central Command?" she said looking around.

"There," said Oh, pointing up.

Above them sat the Eiffel Tower, floating in mid-air and with a large, purple Boov ball on the top. As Tip looked around, she could see Boov everywhere. Some walking, some talking, some sat at restaurants eating paintings!

Then, she turned and saw a sign. It was a wanted-style poster with Oh's face on it and symbols that she didn't understand.

"We will never make it through with you looking like that. You'll be recognised straight away. I've got a plan," she said, running back to Slushious.

Tip came back with a make-up bag.

"You need a disguise," she said. Tip took out an eyeliner pencil and leaned towards Oh. As the pencil touched his cheek, Oh stepped back and held up a mirror, looking at the small, black dot on his face.

"You are a genius," he cried. "Who is this strange Boov that I see looking back at me?" Just as he was about to walk out into the crowd, an alarm sounded.

"Attention, all Boov. Five minutes until Gorg ships reach us."

The Boov in the streets began to panic and run for cover.

"Now!" cried Tip, grabbing Oh's arm and running to a nearby Bubble-ship. The pair jumped in and Oh took the controls. Seconds later, they were at the entrance to Central Command.

Oh led the way as they raced through the corridors and into the main computer room. The alarm still sounded a countdown until Gorg arrival.

"Quick, we have less than two minutes," cried Tip. Oh sat at the control panel and opened the Boov email window. He typed in his password and pressed enter.

INCORRECT PASSWORD. TWO ATTEMPTS REMAINING flashed on the screen.

"What's happening?" said Tip. "Why didn't it work?"

"I must have pressed the wrong key," said Oh. He typed again.

INCORRECT PASSWORD. ONE ATTEMPT REMAINING flashed up. Oh looked at the keyboard, puzzled.

"Attention, all Boov, **15** seconds until Gorg arrival." Suddenly, Oh saw a light on at the top of the keyboard. Caps lock was on! He pressed the key and then typed his password. **EMAIL CANCELLED** showed in big, green letters.

"Oh, you did it!" cried Tip, wrapping her arms around him. The alarm sounded a long tone, then a beep, then stopped. Oh continued to tap away at the computer keys.

"Here, Tip, this is the location of your mum," he said, as a hologram appeared in front of them showing a globe of Earth. On it, a red light blinked… in Australia. Tip couldn't believe it. Her mum was all the way across the world in Australia.

Oh uploaded the location to his handheld computer and turned around.

"Come on," said Tip. "Let's get out of here quick."

Tip followed Oh to the entrance and pushed open the doors. Outside was Captain Smek, as well as Kyle and an army of Boov guards.

"Stop, intruders!" cried Captain Smek. Oh stepped forward.

"Please, wait. It is me, Oh. I have cancelled the email. Things can go back to normal."

"You are not Oh," said Kyle. "I know Oh, he looks like all Boov." Oh reached up and wiped the black dot from his face. The Boov crowd gasped and some even fainted.

"It is impossible. It is you," said Kyle, shocked.

"Well, Oh, you may have stopped the email, but you still sent it in the first place," said Captain Smek. "We cannot take a risk that you will not do something silly like this again. Guards, erase him!"

The Boov guards raised their Bubble-guns toward Oh. Tip quickly looked around, trying to find a way to protect her friend, when she saw a large lever hanging down beside her. She pulled it and, suddenly, the floor began to tilt.

"What's going on?" she shouted to Oh.

"You have turned off the gravity. We are turning upside down," cried Oh. "Hold onto something."

The Boov guards began to slide around, reaching for anything they could find. Captain Smek ran as fast as he could to his Bubble-ship and took off.

"Quick, Oh, this way," shouted Tip, climbing onto the frame of the tower.

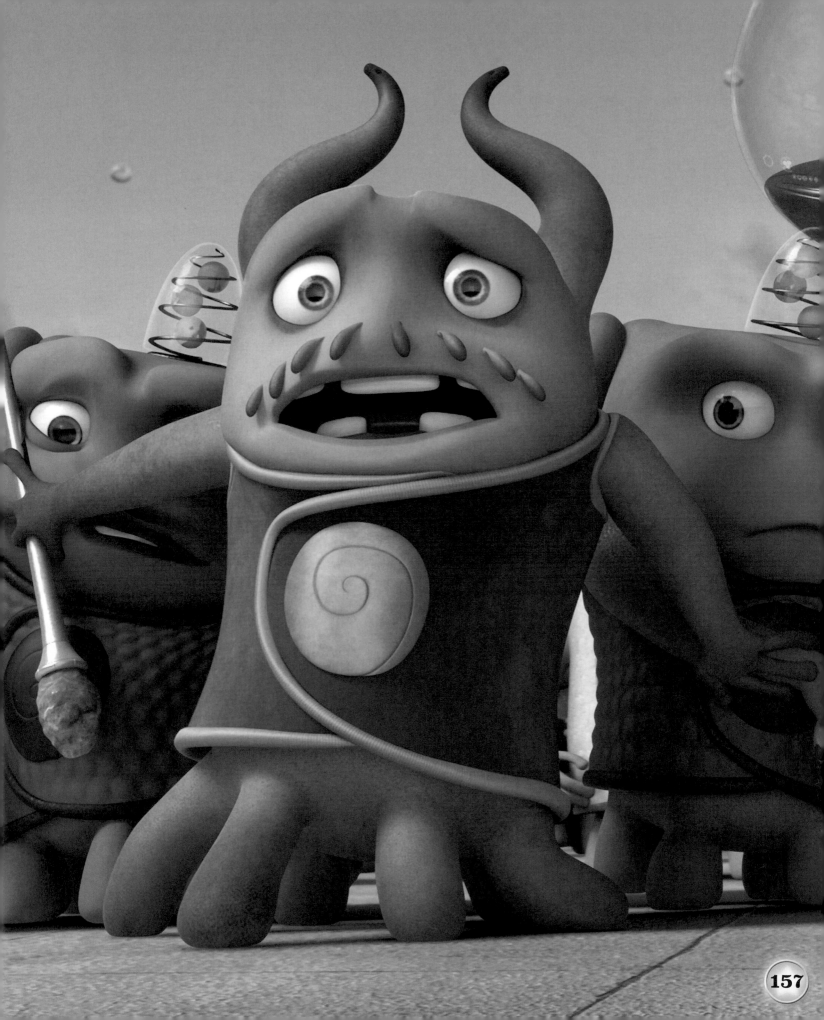

Oh followed Tip and they climbed to the highest point of the tower. As they looked down, they saw that Kyle was chasing after them.

"We have to jump," said Tip, holding onto the tower and leaning out. "Aim for that rooftop." With a giant leap, Tip jumped from the tower, as it swung past a nearby building. Without even thinking, Oh followed her.

The pair got up and looked back to see if Kyle was going to follow them. Just as he leaned forward, the tower picked up speed and he was thrown backwards. Kyle hung onto the tower and watched it swing past the building and away.

Tip and Oh ran back to Slushious. They jumped in and woke up Pig, who was sleeping in the back. They flew up into the clouds and away from Paris. When they reached the ocean, they stopped to take a rest.

"Thank you, Tip. You saved me," said Oh, sheepishly. "I cannot believe that Captain Smek would want me erased. I have always been a loyal Boov."

"Perhaps Captain Smek isn't who you thought, Oh," said Tip. "Perhaps you need to start making your own choices."

"Perhaps humanspersons are not so silly after all," said Oh. "Your bravery saved me."

Oh smiled at Tip and they decided that they should get some sleep. They had a long flight to Australia the next day.

Oh opened his eyes and heard a strange rumbling sound.
He turned his head and looked out of the window.
"Quick, Tip. Wake up! Captain Smek has found us," he said, shaking Tip's arm.
Tip woke up and jumped forward with a start.
"What?" she said. "How?"
Outside, Boov ships surrounded them. As they looked, trying to find a way to escape, they realised that the ships were flying PAST them and into the sky above.
"They aren't after us," said Tip.
"Why are they flying away?"
"The only reason the Boov would run is if the Gorg had come," said Oh, worried.
"We cancelled the email," said Tip. "How would they find us?"
"They must have come into range sooner than expected," said Oh.
"They have followed the signal to Earth and now they have found us. Boov are in danger and it is all my fault."

Suddenly, through the clouds, a large Gorg ship appeared and began to fire at the Boov ships. Before long, more Gorg ships had appeared and a battle between Boov and Gorg had begun.
Tip quickly reached for the keys and started Slushious. Bubbles flew from the back as they began to dart past Boov and Gorg ships.
"This is not good. This is bad," said Oh.
"We are doomed!"

Suddenly, a stray shot hit Slushious and it began to spiral out of control.
"Hold onto something, Oh. We are going down!" cried Tip.

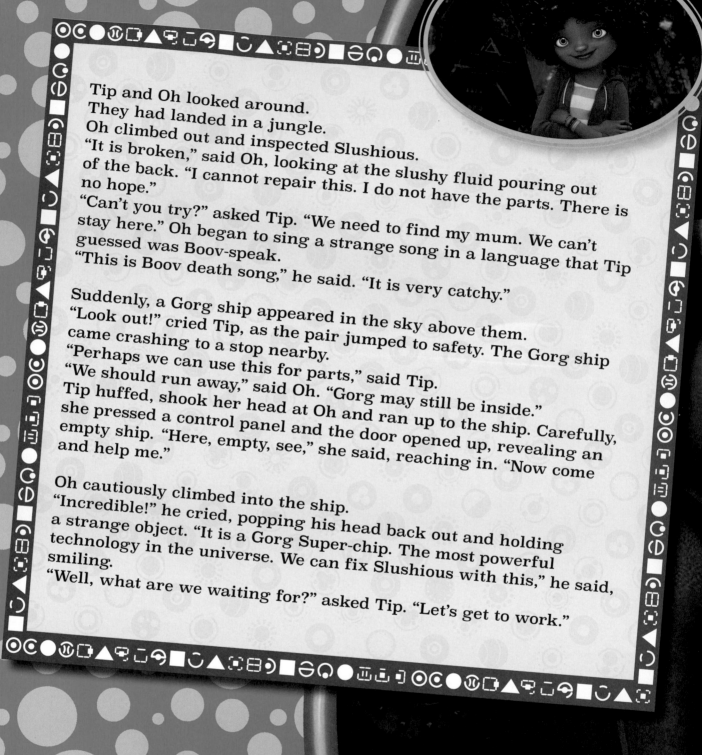

Tip and Oh looked around.

They had landed in a jungle.

Oh climbed out and inspected Slushious.

"It is broken," said Oh, looking at the slushy fluid pouring out of the back. "I cannot repair this. I do not have the parts. There is no hope."

"Can't you try?" asked Tip. "We need to find my mum. We can't stay here." Oh began to sing a strange song in a language that Tip guessed was Boov-speak.

"This is Boov death song," he said. "It is very catchy."

Suddenly, a Gorg ship appeared in the sky above them.

"Look out!" cried Tip, as the pair jumped to safety. The Gorg ship came crashing to a stop nearby.

"Perhaps we can use this for parts," said Tip.

"We should run away," said Oh. "Gorg may still be inside."

Tip huffed, shook her head at Oh and ran up to the ship. Carefully, she pressed a control panel and the door opened up, revealing an empty ship. "Here, empty, see," she said, reaching in. "Now come and help me."

Oh cautiously climbed into the ship.

"Incredible!" he cried, popping his head back out and holding a strange object. "It is a Gorg Super-chip. The most powerful technology in the universe. We can fix Slushious with this," he said, smiling.

"Well, what are we waiting for?" asked Tip. "Let's get to work."

Some time later, Oh and Tip were flying over Australia, following Oh's computer to Tip's mum's last known location.

As they arrived, they could see two large Boov ships with queues of Boov lining up to get aboard.
"Boov escape ships," said Oh. "These are the last hope for safety."

Tip landed Slushious near the larger of the two ships. Oh took the Super-chip from the dashboard and they stepped out.
"Which way?" asked Tip, looking at Oh and the computer.
"This way," said Oh, starting to walk toward the escape ship.
As Tip turned around, she saw that Oh had changed to a dark shade of green.
"You're lying!" she said, shocked. "You changed to the same colour when you lied about having lasers in your eyes back in the shop."
"This ship is the last hope for safety," said Oh. "I just want you to be safe, Tip. You have saved me enough. I can now repay you."
"I can't leave my mum here," said Tip. "I have to find her. Family is the most important thing, Oh. You should do anything to protect them."

Tip turned and ran into the crowd, shouting her mum's name. Oh chased after her, but soon she had disappeared out of sight. Suddenly, everything went dark. A huge Gorg ship had flown overhead and was casting an enormous shadow over the buildings and crowds of Boov below. Oh panicked. He looked at the Gorg ship, then at the crowd where Tip had disappeared and then ran onto the escape ship.

On board, the Boov cowered at the back of the flight deck. In front of them was a huge window and through it they could see the approaching Gorg ship. They were all frozen with fear, helpless and afraid. The flight controls for the ship were positioned just in front of the glass, but no Boov was brave enough to step forward and use them. Oh looked around. If they couldn't fly away then they were definitely all doomed.

Suddenly, Oh saw Captain Smek in the corner of the room. "Captain Smek will save us. He is our brave leader," he shouted. Captain Smek looked up, yelped and covered his eyes with his hand.
"If I cannot see it, then it cannot be real," he muttered, while sobbing and sucking his thumb.

Oh thought back to his time with Tip. He thought of the adventure they had been on and how they had survived because of Tip's bravery. Oh stepped forward. The room full of Boov gasped in disbelief. Oh took another step and another. Soon, Oh was at the control panel, but the Gorg ship was too close. The Boov ship didn't have enough power to escape. They would never make it.

Oh took the Super-chip and wired it into the ship's controls. The needles on the power gauges flew round the dials and a message flashed on-screen...
... POWER AT 500%
Oh pressed the launch button and the Boov ship rocketed into the air, throwing the Boov crowd backwards. Before long, the Boov ship was outside Earth's atmosphere.

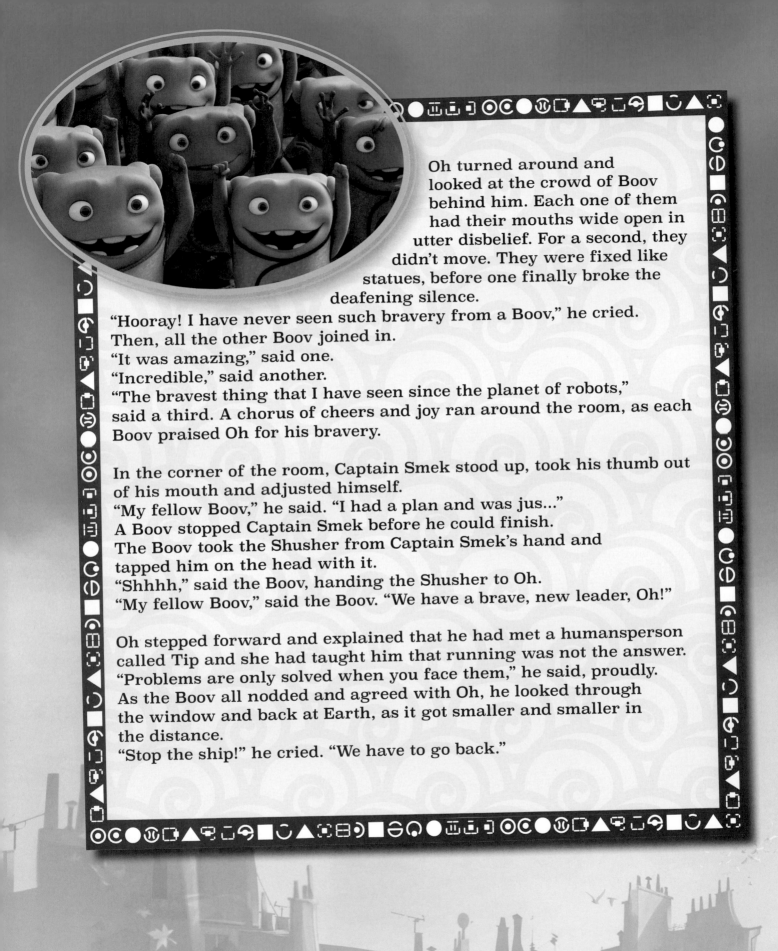

Oh turned around and looked at the crowd of Boov behind him. Each one of them had their mouths wide open in utter disbelief. For a second, they didn't move. They were fixed like statues, before one finally broke the deafening silence.

"Hooray! I have never seen such bravery from a Boov," he cried. Then, all the other Boov joined in.

"It was amazing," said one.

"Incredible," said another.

"The bravest thing that I have seen since the planet of robots," said a third. A chorus of cheers and joy ran around the room, as each Boov praised Oh for his bravery.

In the corner of the room, Captain Smek stood up, took his thumb out of his mouth and adjusted himself.

"My fellow Boov," he said. "I had a plan and was jus..."

A Boov stopped Captain Smek before he could finish. The Boov took the Shusher from Captain Smek's hand and tapped him on the head with it.

"Shhhh," said the Boov, handing the Shusher to Oh.

"My fellow Boov," said the Boov. "We have a brave, new leader, Oh!"

Oh stepped forward and explained that he had met a humansperson called Tip and she had taught him that running was not the answer.

"Problems are only solved when you face them," he said, proudly. As the Boov all nodded and agreed with Oh, he looked through the window and back at Earth, as it got smaller and smaller in the distance.

"Stop the ship!" he cried. "We have to go back."

Meanwhile, in Australia, Tip was barging through crowds of people, holding the photo of her mum. "Have you seen this woman?" she asked random strangers. "It's my mum, I need to find her."

Everyone was too panicked by the huge alien ship to pay Tip any attention. They just ran in different directions, desperately trying to find somewhere to hide.

As Tip rounded a corner, she was pushed by a wave of people and fell to the ground. It was no use. She thought she would never find her mum.

Suddenly, across the road, she saw a familiar face. Tip jumped up and ran across the road. "Oh, you're back!" she cried. "You came back!" Oh smiled. "Hello, Tip," he said. "I realised that I had a promise to keep. You helped me and now I must help you." Oh took out his computer and the pair followed the signal through busy streets of people, before turning a corner. In front of them, a dark-haired woman was running up to people holding a photo. "Have you seen this girl?" she was asking strangers. "It's my daughter. I have to find her. She is called Tip."

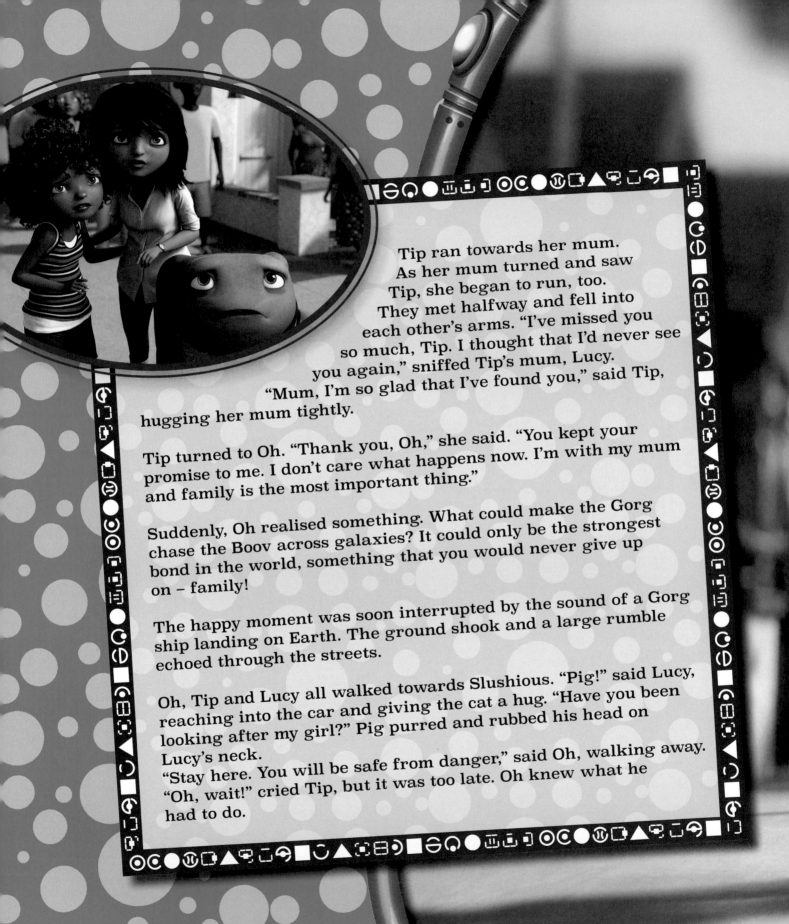

Tip ran towards her mum. As her mum turned and saw Tip, she began to run, too. They met halfway and fell into each other's arms. "I've missed you so much, Tip. I thought that I'd never see you again," sniffed Tip's mum, Lucy. "Mum, I'm so glad that I've found you," said Tip, hugging her mum tightly.

Tip turned to Oh. "Thank you, Oh," she said. "You kept your promise to me. I don't care what happens now. I'm with my mum and family is the most important thing."

Suddenly, Oh realised something. What could make the Gorg chase the Boov across galaxies? It could only be the strongest bond in the world, something that you would never give up on – family!

The happy moment was soon interrupted by the sound of a Gorg ship landing on Earth. The ground shook and a large rumble echoed through the streets.

Oh, Tip and Lucy all walked towards Slushious. "Pig!" said Lucy, reaching into the car and giving the cat a hug. "Have you been looking after my girl?" Pig purred and rubbed his head on Lucy's neck.
"Stay here. You will be safe from danger," said Oh, walking away.
"Oh, wait!" cried Tip, but it was too late. Oh knew what he had to do.

As Oh approached
the huge Gorg ship,
he could feel his legs
go wobbly. Everything inside
him was telling him to run away
from the ship, but he knew that
he couldn't do that. He was the last
hope for this planet called Earth and all the remaining Boov and
humanspersons that were on it. Oh stopped when he reached what
looked like a door and held up the Shusher.

Suddenly, a large hiss sounded, followed by a jet of steam.
The door opened, revealing bright, white light. Oh could make
out a shadow moving inside. From the doorway, a huge, armoured
alien stepped out. Oh was terrified, but stood his ground.
The armoured alien stepped towards Oh, the ground vibrating
with each step it took. When it was near Oh, it stopped and there
was silence.

Oh was so scared, he couldn't speak. Still holding the Shusher,
Oh finally found some courage.
"Gorg, I know what you have been searching for," he said.
"For centuries, you have chased my species across galaxies and we
have never known why until this day. It is because of this."
Oh shook the Shusher gently. "I understand now what the most
important thing in the universe is and that is because of the people
who live on this planet."

The Gorg took one step towards Oh and then stopped.
Suddenly, there was a loud hiss like before. Oh was scared.

The Gorg alien raised its arms and pieces of the suit began to slide about, moving up and away from its body. Layer after layer moved and reorganised until, eventually, only a tiny alien was left. Oh stood in amazement. This was the Gorg that Boov have feared for so many centuries? Destroyer of planets, the thing of Boov nightmares for as long as Oh could remember?

The Gorg stepped forward once more and carefully took the Shusher from Oh's hand. It twisted the stone on the end and the top of it popped open. As it did, bright light poured out. Oh had been right, the Gorg just wanted the staff back. The Gorg smiled at the Shusher and then spoke to Oh.

After a brief conversation, it was clear to Oh why the Gorg had been so desperate to get the staff back. It was full of millions of tiny, microscopic Gorg eggs.

Seeing that the Gorg was not going to harm Oh, Tip and her mum ran over to join him.

"What is it?" asked Tip. "What has all of this been about?"

Oh translated what the Gorg had said to him.

"The Gorg is a mother," he said. "Many years ago, when Boov visited the Gorg for a peaceful meeting, Captain Smek got scared and ran away, carrying the Shusher. What Captain Smek did not know, was that the Shusher was the carrier for all of the Gorg babies. Without the Shusher, the Gorg species would have died out and become extinct.

Like you, Tip, the Gorg has just been searching for her family all of this time and, as you taught me, family is the most important thing and a person will stop at nothing to find them. I have explained to the Gorg that we did not know what we had and that this was all a misunderstanding and she has accepted that. She will never trouble the Boov, or humanspersons, anymore."

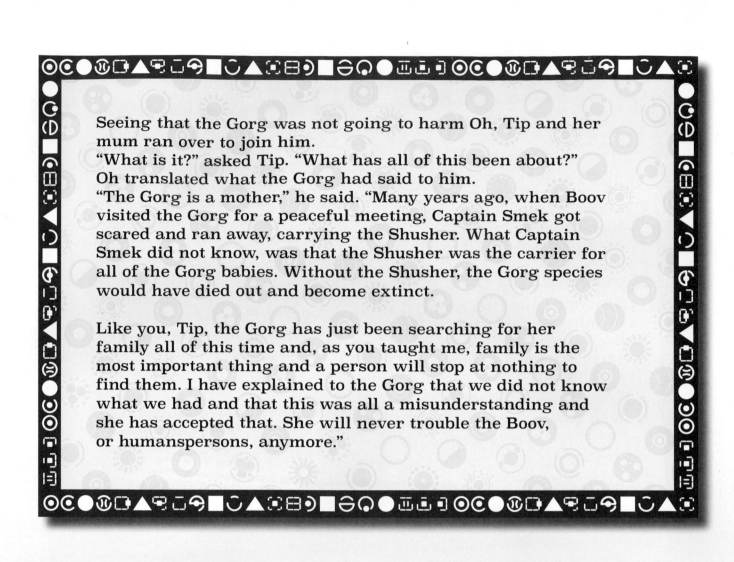

Oh looked at the Gorg and smiled. The Gorg smiled back and turned away, heading back toward its ship.

As Oh, Tip and her mum looked on, the ship door closed and the engines began to roar. In a cloud of dust, the ship lifted off the ground and hovered for a moment, before taking off with a deafening roar and an intense flash of light.

Tip turned to Oh and gave him a huge hug. "I'm so proud of you, Oh," she said. "You've been braver and smarter than anyone that I've ever known. You will be a brilliant leader for all of the Boov." "Thank you," said Oh. "I do not think that we will be seeing her again. Tip, you are safe now." Oh continued. "Thank you, Tip," said Oh. "You have taught me a great deal that I will never forget. I promise."

Boov everywhere began to cheer. "We are saved! Hooray for our brave, new leader! Oh, the Hero Boov."